Loving Without Limits
(*Edenton Bay Romance* Series, Book 3)

Elizabeth Woodrow

ISBN: 979-8-9990697-1-9 (paperback)
ISBN: 979-8-9990697-0-2 (ebook)

Dedication

In Loving Memory

Of

Caitlyn LeeAnn Logan

December 28, 1998 – March 16, 2020

May your light always shine this side of heaven

"Love knows no limit to its endurance, no end to its trust, no fading of its hope; it can outlast anything. It is, in fact, the one thing that still stands when all else has fallen."

—1 Corinthians 13:7-8a (J.B. Phillips New Testament)

Contents

Chapter 1

Wyatt Glover

As I sat in the rocking chair on the front porch of my cabin at Redemption Ranch, I whittled a horse from a piece of wood as dark storm clouds brewed in the distance, mirroring my mood. I thought about the events of the past few weeks. I had attended the funeral of little Quinn Taylor, who was taken from the world way too soon. Quinn and her mother, Emelia, had arrived at the ranch at the end of May. Quinn had just celebrated her fifth birthday before she passed in October. I missed her presence. Her laughter. The sunshine she brought to everyone's day.

I gazed across the dirt road and focused on the grassy plain behind the row of cabins. Blades of grass danced in the wind as my own childhood drifted through my mind. The love everyone had for Quinn made me wonder even more how my own parents could abandon their kid. Drugs made people do things they wouldn't normally do, I guessed. I hoped that's what it was.

When Colt Andrews found me at the bus station in Dallas, Texas, I was fifteen years old. I had been living there for a week or two but had been on the streets for two years. I was a homeless teenager, and I looked every bit of it, too.

Colt told me about a place he had and asked if I wanted to

go. I didn't hesitate to say yes. Even though it had sounded too good to be true, I thought it had to be better than where I was or had been. He said the only way to do it, though, was the right way and have a judge make Colt my legal guardian. Redemption Ranch and all the people that lived there, including my best friend, Caitlyn Logan, had been the only constants in my life since then. Maybe even ever.

The wind whistled and tousled my hair as Colt hollered breathlessly, drawing me from my thoughts. "Wyatt, hurricane's comin'! We gotta get the ranch ready!"

I dropped the block of wood and jumped from my chair, swiping my knife across my thigh to remove wood shavings as I fell into step with Colt. "Let's get to it, then. How long do we have?"

"Not long. Weatherman says it's changed course, and it should hit us by tomorrow sometime."

Tomorrow? My pulse revved, and a knot formed in my throat.

As if reading my mind, Colt picked up the pace. Both of us were now jogging down the path to the stable, my ankles wobbling in my cowboy boots. I could only imagine Colt's were doing the same.

"Guess we should've gotten started a little sooner," Colt noted. "But they originally said we had until later in the week. They still aren't sure exactly how bad it's gonna be yet. We'll have to keep a close eye on the news and just prepare for the worst. At this point, though, they're sayin' evacuation isn't needed, so that's good." Colt glanced over at me, concern etched in his lowered brow. "It's a category three, and we've seen worse, but it could get worse also. So, I want to take every precaution possible. Just to be safe."

I'd been through a few hurricanes since coming to Edenton,

North Carolina, but they'd just been like bad rainstorms. Tornadoes in Texas had been much worse.

Colt stood just outside the stable where everyone from the ranch had already gathered as this was always our emergency meeting place. He jumped onto the picnic table and cupped his hands around his mouth. "Okay, everyone. Listen up!"

The air fell silent as a gust of wind swept through, taking Colt's Stetson hat with it. Jon caught it before it blew away and handed it back to him. "Thanks, Jon. We need to get ready for this hurricane that's brewin'. The weatherman says it should be here by tomorrow between 12 and 2 p.m. That is, if the storm continues on its current path. It could change, but we need to be ready, and we have a lot to get done with not a lot of time to do it. If we work together, I know we can accomplish everythin'." Colt handed Callie a small stack of papers. "Callie is passin' 'round the list I made of all the things that need to be done. We'll divide up into groups of two and assign each group some jobs, but if ya get done, please go 'round and see if anyone else needs help, or if no one is workin' on somethin' from the list, pick another task."

I noticed Colt said groups of two but realized that you can't make an even number out of odds. I glanced at the paper, each line filled with a job. We were going to be here well into the night. But ranch work had no opening or closing time. You worked until the work was done.

"We'll just have to keep watchin' the reports in case things change," Colt continued. "Callie and I also want everyone to plan on stayin' at the house startin' tonight. Just like every other hurricane situation we've had. With that said, Jon and Spencer," Colt pointed to the two men, "get the horses put out to pasture. That has always been a safe place for them, away from trees that could potentially fall on them. Also, be sure to put the water barrels out there."

Colt lifted his hat off, wiped his forehead with his arm, and then returned the hat to his head. "All the horses have had their appropriate vaccines, so we're good there. Oh, and make sure to put their ID bands around their necks. I forgot to put that on the list. Get the large barrels out and fill them with water, and put one on each end of the corral."

He turned to me. "Wyatt, while they're doin' that, you get all the hay into the stable and onto pallets with the rest of the bales and cover them with tarps. Also, check the feed barrels and make sure we have enough for at least seven days per horse. If we don't, let me know, and we can go into town to the Feed Barn."

Colt inhaled deeply as he glanced up at the changing sky before instructing the other pairs of two. Before we all dispersed, he said, "If I've forgotten to mention anythin', just check the list. Thanks, everyone. See ya back at the house later."

Not having a partner was something I was still getting used to. Austin was typically my partner, but he was kicked out of the ranch when he tried to put the moves on Emelia, and Caitlyn had left for college in Indiana a few months before. I didn't miss Austin as much as I missed her. It was rough without her close by. More than I thought possible. I worried about her because of her diabetes and being so far away from home. Away from me. I would never confess any of that to her, though. She always said she just wanted to be normal and not have to deal with her illness, so I did my best not to talk about it. I missed my best friend. A sharp pain radiated through my heart. I ground my fist into my chest in hopes it would diminish the pain.

I didn't have a girlfriend because, well, I didn't look like the rest of the guys on the ranch—muscular and fit. My body was extra chubby. I was scrawny when I was homeless. Until I got to the ranch, that is. After not having a home-cooked meal for, well, my entire life, having someone who cooked as well as Richard Alan helped me pack on the pounds over the years.

As I stood in front of the pile of hay bales inside the stable, I scratched the back of my head. It was going to be a hefty chore without a partner, but I really couldn't complain. Life at the ranch was the best. Even on the worst day, ranch life was so much better than the life I would've had if I'd stayed in Dallas. That much I knew for sure.

Once I had the bales on the pallets that were inside the barn, I brought in the bales that were outside and stacked them on top of the others. After I placed the last bale on top, I covered them with the large, blue tarp. I grabbed some ropes from a hook on the wall and put them into the metal grommets at each corner before tying the ropes to the pallets. I hoped that would keep the tarp from blowing away and taking the hay with it.

With the tarp firmly in place, I went to check the feed barrels on the backside of the stable. I pried off the lids with the crowbar lying on top of them. Each barrel, at full capacity, held about 600 pounds of feed. We had eight horses. Each horse would eat about nine pounds of feed per day. So, if my math was correct (and let's face it, math was *not* my strong subject in school), we had to have around 500 pounds of feed for the seven days. One barrel was completely full, and the other was almost three-quarters full. We were good to go. I laid the lid back on each barrel, removed the mallet hanging from the wall, and tapped the barrels shut, making sure the lids were securely in place. I hung the mallet back on the wall and placed the crowbar across the top of the barrels.

"Everything has its place and needs to be put back where it belongs for the next person," Colt's voice ran through my mind. It was ingrained because, when I first got here, that was one of the things I had the most trouble doing. Maybe it was just having rules in general. I shrugged off the memory and hustled to take some hay bales to the trough we had out in the open fields for things like this. It allowed the horses to eat in case we weren't able to get out there because of the weather.

"Colt, anythin' else I can do?" I asked, brushing my hands on the sides of my pants after I returned to the front of the stable and found Colt at this truck.

"Oh, hey, Wyatt." He peered over his shoulder. "Do we need any hay or feed?" Colt grunted as he laid out a couple of boards that I assumed were for the windows of the cabins.

"Nope. We're good on both."

"Great." Colt let a board fall to the bed of his truck.

"Need any help with those?" I motioned toward the boards.

"Sure. I could use some. I'm gettin' these boards loaded up to take to the cabins. Since everyone is stayin' at the house, Callie went to the grocery store to pick up some things we're runnin' low on. She talked Emelia into goin' with her. Hopefully, Callie can talk her into stayin' at the house, too. Luke has been tryin' to coax her but hasn't had much luck." Colt wiped his brow with his handkerchief before stuffing it into his back pocket.

"That should be fun." My voice dripped with sarcasm.

"It'll be fine. You should be used to it by now." Colt chuckled. "Let's get movin'. We've got a lot of boards to put up, and we're goin' to be runnin' out of daylight in the next couple of hours."

Colt slammed the tailgate shut and climbed into the driver's seat. I scrambled to the passenger door and jumped in before he took off down the dirt road to the cabins. "Let's do the individual cabins first," Colt suggested, "since most of those are occupied. Then, we can do the family cabins," he said as we pulled up to the first cabin.

As I set my feet on the ground, I glanced over at the cabin across from our starting point. I stood in front of Emelia's old cabin—the one she had lived in with Quinn. My breath hitched as I half expected Quinn to race out the door and leap into my arms. I swiped at the wetness that had formed in the corner of my eye and cleared my throat of the lump that had formed.

Just before Thanksgiving, two weeks after Quinn's funeral, Emelia moved from that cabin to an individual one. She said she couldn't stay in it anymore. It was too much for her. Her boyfriend, Luke Herring, and I helped move her things. I think that was up there on the list of the hardest things I've done in my life. I wish I'd known what else I could've done for her, but I felt helpless. Colt's wife, Callie, had packed up what was left of Quinn's things the day after Emelia moved. Emelia insisted, though, that everything be taken to a battered women's shelter. Everything except the little brown bear Luke had won for Quinn at the fair. If she hadn't buried Horsey with Quinn, I know she would have kept him, too. After all, he was Quinn's absolute favorite stuffed animal.

The ranch felt different without Quinn running around. She had quickly become everyone's little sidekick. I loved the time I'd gotten to spend with her over the summer. Especially teaching her how to spit watermelon seeds. That seemed like a lifetime ago already. I rubbed the back of my head as a smile formed on my lips at the memory of Quinn successfully spitting that seed and being so proud of herself.

I walked to the back of Colt's truck.

"'Bout time," Colt said with a chuckle. "What're ya grinnin' 'bout?" He let the tailgate down and removed the first board.

I startled at the sound of his voice as I hadn't fully left the memory. Shaking my head, I returned to the present. "Oh. I was just thinkin' 'bout Quinn."

"Yeah." Colt sighed. "It's not the same without her here, huh?"

"It's really not. She was one of a kind. Wish I knew what more I could do for Emelia."

"I think we all feel that way. Hopefully, she'll come to the house. Not sure how much luck Callie and Luke will have with that, though." Colt shrugged. "All we can really do is be there whenever she needs somethin'."

"I hope they succeed. Maybe it'll help just by us all bein' together." I shrugged.

"Yeah. Maybe so." Colt sighed as he glanced at the trees bending to the wind. "Well, these boards aren't gonna put themselves up. After we get them secured, we can head to the house. Then, we just have to wait and see if or when this storm hits." Colt lifted another board and let it fall to the ground before picking up the last one from the bed of his truck.

As we boarded up the windows, the wind made it difficult to hold the planks against the frames. My mind managed to wander to Chipmunk. I silently chuckled at the nickname I'd given Caitlyn. Gosh, even that seemed like a lifetime ago. It was shortly after my arrival in town. Colt and the guys had had a bonfire, and of course, the Logans were there. We played a game of Chubby Bunny. Caitlyn had shoved so many marshmallows in her mouth that I said she looked like a chipmunk, and that had been her nickname ever since. Of course, I was the only one who called her that. I wasn't sure if anyone else even knew about it, so I tried not to call her that when other people were around.

I missed her. More than I ever thought possible. We had been best friends ever since that night at the bonfire. It had only been four years, but it was one of the best relationships I'd ever had in my life. Not seeing her every day anymore was hard to wrap my head around. I just hoped I'd survive. A bit overdramatic, I know, but being abandoned by my parents left me a little sensitive to that kind of change.

"Well, that's all done. That wind sure didn't take it easy on us, did it?" Colt gazed out over the cabins with his hands planted on his waist.

The wind had picked up even more than when we first started. The sun was setting in the sky—what had been visible behind the storm clouds, anyway. The crisp, clean scent that fills the air before an impending storm was calming under the chaotic circumstances.

"It sure didn't." I wiped my forehead with the back of my hand as the first raindrops pelted my head.

"Ya ready to get to the house?" Colt asked as he turned to me before lifting his eyes to the sky.

"Let me grab my bag, and I'll be ready."

After returning from my cabin, we piled into the truck and jostled down the road in silence. Wasn't much to say. Hurricanes always held the potential to do a lot of damage, but we never knew how much one of them would leave until it had already passed through. The ranch had been lucky so far. None of the hurricanes I'd experienced had ever caused too much damage, or at least none that we hadn't been able to fix ourselves. Would this one prove to be the same?

Everyone was already at the house when we arrived. The first person I noticed as we walked into the living room was Emelia. Relief flooded me. *So glad she decided to stay here with everyone.*

Emelia was sitting off in the corner of the couch next to the wall-to-wall bookshelf. It was as if she wanted to be alone in the crowded room. If I had to guess, anyway.

Even though the house was huge, with everyone there, it felt a little cramped. At least we would know everyone was safe, though. I glanced around the room as everyone chatted away. The house was the first that had ever felt like home to me. I had lived there with Colt in the beginning. All the men in the room, and then Callie when she had arrived, made me feel like I finally had a family. It felt amazing to have one for the first time in my life—that I could remember, anyway.

"Hey, Emelia," I greeted her as I sat at the other end of the couch.

"Hey, Wyatt," she responded quietly. "How're you doing?" Just like Emelia, to be going through so much and still asking how I was doing.

"I'm okay." I took in a breath. "I'd ask how you're doin', but I'm sure you're sick of everyone askin' ya that by now."

"Yeah." She twisted the bottom of her shirt with her fingers.

"I'm really glad you're here with us."

A slight smile creased Emelia's lips before disappearing. "Thank you, Wyatt. Very sweet of you to say."

We sat in silence after that. I didn't really know what else to say, but I wanted her to know that I was there for her, even though she had Callie and Luke.

My eyes moved around the room once more. Everyone was scattered about, chatting with each other. Colt had gone straight to Callie and wrapped his arm around her shoulder as she talked with Richard. Spencer, Jon, and Luke were in a corner of the room in deep conversation. *Wonder what they're talkin' 'bout.*

Another gray couch, like the one Emelia and I were sitting

on, sat directly across from us, a darker gray chair at one end. The chair looked like it had a fluffy cushion. I bet it felt like sitting on a cloud. It was a new chair, so I hadn't had the chance to sit in it and find out. Along the entire wall were white bookshelves filled with books. No doubt those were Callie's. I'd never seen Colt with a book before, only ranch or horse magazines. It was a cozy room, really.

* * *

The next day, the dismal sky opened up. As we hunkered down to wait out the storm, the torrential downpour bombarded the roof, and the wind slapped against the siding and the boards over the windows. Emelia jumped. Every. Single. Time. No doubt she was still reeling from the death of Quinn as well as healing from her abusive ex-boyfriend. Every time she flinched, Luke was right there to bring her comfort.

"Hurricane Micah has been downgraded from a category three to a category one," the weatherman reported. "There has been significant damage and flooding across the state due to the high winds. We will certainly see more rainfall and high winds over the next few days. I'm sorry I don't have a better forecast for you. Jack, back to you."

I guess we just have to wait. I sighed.

That night, we were all seated around the table, playing a round of Rummy. Before I knew what I was doing, I blurted out, "I wonder what Quinn would be doin' right now." As soon as the words left my mouth, my gaze fell on Emelia, and I bit my bottom lip. Hard. "Sorry, Emelia. I wasn't thinking."

When Emelia's eyes met mine, they were glassy. She reached her hand out to me. With a crackle in her voice, she said, "You don't need to be sorry, Wyatt. I was wondering the same thing."

"What is everyone's favorite memory with her in it?" I inquired. "Mine was teachin' her how to spit watermelon seeds and helpin' her swim at the Fourth of July Festival." I smiled.

"And teachin' her about faith as small as mouse poop, if I remember correctly," Luke added with a hearty chuckle, which caused a ripple of laughs. Even Emelia laughed. What a sweet sound that was.

Colt laid down a card in the discard pile and chimed in, "I think my favorites were when she helped me fix the fence and when she was my copilot for the hayride at the Harvest Festival. She had wanted to go faster and faster until I told her everyone would fall out if I did."

I peeked over at Emelia to see the smallest smile on her lips as a couple of tears dropped to her cheeks.

Jon laid down a set of three eights and a run of jack, queen, and king of spades before discarding a two of hearts.

"All of my moments with Quinn were my favorite," Luke said. "She was my best girl." He sniffed and covered a cough with his forearm. "But the one that sticks out the most was when I gave her those pink cowgirl boots and that white hat." His voice cracked.

"She loved those boots," Emelia whispered, her eyes on her folded hands in her lap. "Thank you all for sharing these moments. And thank you for loving her as much as you all did. It's no one's fault what happened." She looked up at Luke and laid her hand on his. "I don't regret coming here to the ranch. I just wish we would've found you all sooner so Quinn could have experienced more of what you all gave her the last few months of her life."

As the dam broke, Emelia stood from her place at the table. Her chair's legs screeched across the wood floor, and her sobs consumed the room. She raced from the room with Luke chasing after her. Watching the love they had for each other grow deeper and deeper every day was something I hoped to have with someone someday.

I hoped that someone would be Caitlyn. But first, I had to get up the courage to tell her how I really felt. I didn't want to lose her as my best friend, but I also didn't want to lose her to another guy. She was much too good for the likes of me, though. She deserved only the best. But my heart ached any time I thought about her with someone else.

The lights flickered before the house filled with darkness.

"The generator should kick on in a few minutes," Colt reassured us.

Silence filled the air.

"And there they are," Colt said as the lights illuminated the room once again. "Hopefully, this rain will dissipate tomorrow or at least slow down some. Either way, we'll need to feed the horses in the mornin'."

I hoped so, too.

* * *

The rain lasted five days. Okay, so it was only three nights and two days. But it felt like five days. While I loved everyone at the house like my flesh and blood family, I longed for the solitude of my own cabin.

As soon as the rain stopped the next morning, I wanted to dart off and hide out in my cabin for a few days, but there was work to be done. Colt, Luke, Spencer, Jon, and I went out to check for damage.

We were luckier than other places we'd heard about on the news. There were three places in the fencing where the posts had uprooted and fallen over, a couple of fallen trees, and flooding in some low areas. All of the horses were accounted for as Colt and I led each into the stable and checked them over for any wounds or injuries.

Warrior was the hardest to coax back into the stable. He wouldn't budge for either of us. "Guess it's time to get Callie out here." Colt surrendered, pulling his phone from his pocket. "Hey, babe. Could you come help with Warrior? . . . Yeah, he won't move for us." Colt placed his hand on his waist. "Okay. See you in a few."

"It's okay, boy," I attempted to reassure Warrior. "Callie's on her way. The storm's over now."

"I'm really surprised he didn't run away during the storm," Colt said, coming to stand next to us.

As Callie approached, Warrior trotted over to her. "Hey, boy. Did the storm scare you?" She ran her hand down the side of his face. Then, she wrapped her fingers around the lead rope. "Come on. Let's get you back where you will feel safe, my sweet boy."

"Colt, I'll go help Spencer with the fallen trees," I said.

"Sounds good. Once we get Warrior settled, I'll go help with the fencin'."

Later that evening, I shuffled to my cabin and inhaled a deep breath. *Home. Silence.* That cabin had been my home since I turned eighteen the year before. After Colt had gotten guardianship of me, he said he understood I'd lived most of my life on my own but that I had to live in the house with him until I was an adult.

On my eighteenth birthday, Colt handed me the keys to my cabin. He said that because I was a man and had his trust, he was giving me my own cabin. He told me that if that trust were ever broken, I'd have to move back into the main house. I'd done everything in my power since to keep that trust. So far, I'd succeeded.

I kicked off my boots and set them by the door before making my way to the bedroom. I closed my eyes and sighed. *We didn't check the cabins for damage. Tomorrow. Bed, how I've missed you.* I toppled onto the mattress, without care or concern about getting into my pajamas or under the covers.

Chapter 2

Caitlyn Logan

"**M**om! Dad! Dyl!" I called out, letting the screen door clack behind me and dropping my bags in the entryway. "Anyone here? I'm home!"

I'd just arrived home, unannounced, from Indiana University, where I'd spent my first semester away from home. I'd wanted to come home for Thanksgiving, but because I came home to attend Quinn's funeral, I needed to make up time in my classes. Then, the storm hit, which forced me to stay put longer.

"Mom?" I called out again as I stepped into the kitchen. *Where are they?* "Dad!" I hollered as I strode down the hall to Mom and Dad's room.

The idea of talking to Mom and Dad about something I'd been struggling with since just after Quinn's funeral had my stomach churning. I hoped they wouldn't be too mad or disappointed in me. For that matter, Uncle Colt, Aunt Callie, and Wyatt, too.

I stuck my head into their bedroom. Empty. *They must be at the café.*

With a furrowed brow and pouty lip, I sulked back to the door to retrieve my bags and hauled them upstairs to my room. I tossed them on my bed and headed back down the stairs and out the door. My parents' business, Courageous Café and Bakery, was only a few blocks away from where we lived, so I decided to walk.

Wendy, who lived down the street, jogged toward me, oblivious to the world around her as she belted out the tune that was streaming from the earbuds in her ears. How her lungs could handle singing and jogging at the same time amazed me. As she twirled in a circle, I did my best to anticipate which way she would move on the sidewalk. I moved out of the way just before she would have collided with me. She jogged in place as she pulled the earbud out of her left ear, and pink hue appeared on her cheeks. "Oh, Caitlyn! I'm so sorry. Didn't see you there. Welcome home."

Wendy tucked the earbud back in her ear and sped off to finish her run before I could even respond. I shook my head and giggled. Some things never change.

Glancing back at the only house I'd ever lived in, a smile spread across my face. I'd never tire of that teal house with white trim. I loved the screened-in porch on the side of the house. It was my favorite place to sit on a cool afternoon, wrapped up in a fuzzy blanket, sprawled out on the gray, fluffy couch with nothing more than a good book. And the wrought iron bench on the front porch. That bench held so many memories with Wyatt.

As I continued down the road to the café, my stomach was tied in knots. I wasn't sure how my parents were going to take the news. I was so lost in my anxiety-ridden thoughts, I hadn't noticed Angus, the blue-nosed Pitbull, had come out to greet me. His deep, snarly bark snapped me out of my daze.

"Oh, hey there, Angus. How are ya, boy?" I asked, strolling up to the white picket fence.

At the sound of my voice, Angus flopped his front paws on

the fence, tongue out, begging for a pet.

"I missed you, too." I giggled as I patted the top of his head. "You're such a good boy, aren't ya?" I sighed. "I'd better get goin'. The conversation won't have itself. I'll see ya later, Angus."

Angus removed his paws from the fence as if he understood every word I had said. Then, he sauntered around his light gray, Tudor-style house to his backyard.

Standing in front of the glass door with *Courageous Café and Bakery* stenciled on it, I took in a deep breath and then exhaled sharply. The jingle bells announced my arrival before I was fully inside.

The scent of coffee and baked goods filled the air and had my mouth watering. But to have one would require me to take my insulin, and I was too nervous for that. Oh, how I'd missed those smells. I inhaled as deeply as I could so the smells would stay for as long as possible.

I stopped at the wall where Joshua 1:9 was painted in different colors. *Be Strong and Courageous!* I glided my fingertips over the words as I read them in my mind. *I'm gonna need a lot of both!*

"Sis? What're you doing here?" Mom exclaimed as she came from the kitchen and ran around the long white counter with her arms outstretched.

"I came home a little early to surprise everyone."

"Mission accomplished. But it's a happy surprise."

The warmth of Mom's embrace almost brought me to tears. Being enveloped in her arms always made me feel safe. It was a space I always hoped I'd have. I didn't want to disappoint her or Dad. Ever.

"What's all the commotion out here?" Dad asked, heading out from the kitchen. He smiled. His smile always lit up his whole face as well as the room he was standing in. It made me smile, too. Every single time. He wrapped his arms around me tightly. "Sis, what're you doing here?"

"Surprise!" I had hoped my voice would sound more joyful, but it fell short. "There *is* something I need to tell you both, too."

The timer on the oven sounded. I closed my eyes and inhaled deeply. *Saved by the bell.*

"Ooh. We need to get that out of the oven," Dad said. "Come to the kitchen and tell us what's on your mind." He made his way back to the ovens.

Mom grabbed my hand and dragged me to the kitchen. The route was very familiar as I'd traced those steps every day of my childhood: the silver ovens for baking on one side of the long island in the middle of the room and the fryer and black grill top for food on the other side.

After Dad removed the trays of bread from the oven, he turned his attention to me. "So, what is it? You know you can tell us anything."

I closed my eyes and basked in the aroma of the freshly baked bread—one of my favorite scents in the bakery—as I summoned the courage to speak.

Dad joined Mom on the opposite side of the island that ran almost the entire width of the kitchen. He wiped some flour off part of the white marble before resting on his elbows.

"Well." I twisted my clammy hands at my waist. I gulped and squeezed my eyes shut before ripping off the band-aid and blurting out, "I don't think I want to be a nurse anymore. And I withdrew from classes before coming home."

Mom's mouth dropped open, and her eyes grew wide. *Uh oh.*

"What? What do you mean?" she asked. "You've wanted

to be a nurse since your diagnosis, so you could help kids just like you." She rushed around the island and wrapped an arm around my shoulder. "Are you sure?"

I peered up into Mom's eyes that had returned to their normal size. I expected to see disappointment, but instead, what resided there was concern.

I exhaled. "Well, I want to come home and be an EMT and eventually a paramedic. I feel like if I'd been at the fair that night and was trained, maybe Quinn would still be alive. I want to help people *in* the emergency, not after. I have been prayin' about this since Quinn . . ." I couldn't bring myself to finish that sentence. Quinn had meant so much to me. She was like my little sister.

"I also want to come home to teach dance," I continued. "You already know it's one of the things I love to do. And I miss everyone so much."

"But you couldn't wait to go to IU," Dad finally chimed in. "Don't get me wrong, we'd love to have you back home, but we just want to make sure you make the right decision. For you, that is."

"I feel like God has led me to this place. I didn't make this decision lightly. Like I said, I withdrew from school before I came home. I feel very at peace about it. I just hope neither of you is disappointed in me." My lip quivered as tears pooled at the corners of my eyes.

Mom squeezed me. "Disappointed? Oh, Sis. We could never be disappointed in you. You need to do whatever it is that's going to make you happy. We know Quinn meant a lot to you. If you believe this is what God is telling you to do, then you have to do it. The door will either be open for you or shut, but you won't know until you knock. Your dad and I are always here for you. It will be wonderful to have you home. I will rest easier knowing you are here."

Dad joined us on the other side of the island and engulfed us in a hug.

"What's goin' on in here?" My brother's voice killed the silence. "Hugs without me, I see."

"Sis is here!" Mom exclaimed.

"I see that. Ya missed me too much, didn't ya?" Dyl grinned as he opened his arms for a hug.

I fell into them and wrapped my arms around him. It felt so good to be home. While being away on my own was nice, and a bit of fun, nothing felt better than being with my family and friends.

Speaking of friends, I needed to go see Cowboy. Cowboy was my nickname for Wyatt—for obvious reasons. We had been best friends since I was fourteen and he was fifteen. There was something about him that drew me in from the first moment I met him. He had kindness in his eyes, even after everything he'd been through. I always enjoyed our time together. No matter what we were doing, he had a way of making me feel safe and secure and cared about.

"I'm gonna go surprise Wyatt." I never called him Cowboy around other people. It was just for us. And I didn't want to embarrass him.

Mom and Dad grinned and glanced at each other.

What the heck is that about? I rolled my eyes before strolling back home to drive to Redemption Ranch.

The ranch was more than just a ranch. It was a sanctuary for broken people and broken horses to be restored by God in whatever way they needed. It was owned and run by Uncle Colt and Aunt Callie. They weren't really my uncle and aunt, but they were so much more than family friends. They *were* my family. I wondered how they would take my news. I sucked my bottom lip into my mouth.

Pulling up to the stable, I parked near the door and scanned my surroundings as I stepped out of my car. No one was in sight. The paddock was empty. I breathed in the fresh first-of-December air. Until hay and manure hit my nose. Scrunching my nose, trying to get rid of the scent, I coughed. Forgot about that.

I strode inside the stable, where I found Callie grooming Warrior. He was my favorite horse, but I would never tell the others. Warrior was covered in scars from being beaten with a whip. His outside was the way many of us were on the inside, beaten and scarred. Just like Warrior needed a doctor and medicine to heal his wounds, we needed the medicine of the one Physician who heals *all* wounds: Jesus. Having dealt with diabetes for the years I had, my mind had been battered and bruised almost as much as, if not more so than, my body. But I knew my God is greater than my disease.

"Hey, Aunt Callie. How are ya?" I finally spoke up.

"Caitlyn! What are you doing here?" She dropped the brush and tugged me into her embrace.

"I'm home for Christmas break, and there is something I wanted to talk to you and Uncle Colt about. Can ya let me know when ya both have some time? I'm gonna go see Wyatt. Any idea where he is?"

"Sure. When I'm done with Warrior, I'll go see what Colt is doing. I believe Wyatt is still out in the corral with Flash and Minnie." Aunt Callie nodded in that direction.

"Minnie and Flash?" My brows scrunched in confusion. I hadn't heard those names before.

"Yeah. They joined us not too long ago. Right after the storms, actually. They were abandoned by their owners." Aunt Callie shook her head. "I'll never understand how people can be so cruel."

Even after all Aunt Callie had been through in her life—the death of her parents when she was sixteen and the unspeakable things her aunt did to her—she still had the kindest heart.

I smiled. "Can't wait to meet 'em."

"Go on. They're gorgeous." Aunt Callie returned my smile and nodded toward the corral.

I rushed out the back of the stable. It wasn't until Wyatt came into view that I realized how much I'd truly missed him. I stepped up onto the first rung of the wooden fence surrounding the corral. Placing my hand above my eyes to shield them from the sun, I drank in the sight of Wyatt interacting with the pair of horses. My eyes had been parched from the lonely desert of not seeing him every day.

Wyatt was all cowboy with his Wrangler jeans, button-down plaid shirt, dusty and well-worn brown boots, and dark brown and faded cowboy hat. That hat was always perched on top of his head, his light brown hair barely visible under it. His eyes, even though I couldn't see them in that moment, were as clear as the blue sky above.

My attention turned to the horses. I had no clue which horse was Flash and which one was Minnie. One was dark brown. Its tail, mane, and lower legs were as black as the sky at midnight. The only white on its body was a patch between its eyes. The other horse was one of the most beautiful horses I'd ever seen. Chestnut Brown covered the sides of its head, down its front, and along its underbelly, with a strip up each side. The rest of it was white. The horse's mane was the same dark brown, and its tail was a lighter shade of brown—at least against the sunlight it was.

A smile spread across Wyatt's face when he noticed me. He started in my direction. I entered the corral before jogging over to him and jumping straight into his arms. *Don't ever let go.* I held on tighter, and so did he.

"What're ya doin' here?" His voice was full of surprise.

"Hi to you, too, Cowboy." I giggled and slipped out of his arms. A shiver ran through my body. "You're the fourth person to ask me that. I'm home. I was gonna come home sooner, but the storm hit, and I thought I should wait it out."

"I'm so glad you're home, Chipmunk. And just in time for the Kickoff to Christmas Festival."

I almost swooned at the sound of the nickname he'd given me. I hated it but loved it at the same time. But I'd missed hearing it over the time I'd been gone. We had mostly texted each other, with an occasional phone call. My heart thudded. *Oh, how I've missed this man.*

"I know." I smiled and shoved my hands in my front pockets. "My most favorite time of the year. And not because our birthdays are at the end of the month. So, tell me about these horses. They're gorgeous. Aunt Callie said somethin' 'bout them bein' abandoned?"

Wyatt's gaze fell to the ground. I knew what he was thinking before his words escaped his lips. "Yeah. Just like me."

I laid my hand on his arm and gently squeezed. What could I really say to him? To ease his pain? To comfort him? I couldn't find the words.

"But they are definitely gorgeous. What kind of people could leave them behind?" Wyatt asked.

"Awful people. That's who."

"They were so thin when they arrived. You can still see their ribs pokin' through, but not as bad as when they first got here." Wyatt paused. "Colt said it was time I had my own horse and gave Flash to me."

Wyatt's lips formed the smile I loved so much. A fuzzy

feeling warmed my heart. Uncle Colt didn't give horses to people just because. He gave them to people he knew worked hard, were people he could put his trust in, and who would love the horse the way it deserved to be loved. I could tell it meant the world to Wyatt.

"I've never had people believe in me so much in my whole life. It makes me feel good to know Colt thinks enough of me to give me Flash. He's the brown one, by the way."

"That's awesome. I'm so happy for you. You deserve it so much." I coughed, because if I'd kept going, I might have said too much. *Change the subject. Fast.* "So, how bad was the storm? Did it do much damage around the ranch?"

"It didn't end up bein' more than a few days of a thunderstorm. Heavy and loud but didn't do a lot of damage. Thank goodness. There were some fallen trees, fencin' that got knocked down in a few places, some roof shingles off a couple of cabins. But all-in-all, it wasn't like what we were expectin', which is a good thing."

"Glad it wasn't. How was Thanksgivin'? I was so sad I had to miss it, but I had to make up time in my classes because I came home for the funeral." I sighed. A pain shot through my heart as an image of Quinn danced through my head. I sure did miss her.

"I bet. I imagine Christmas won't be the same either, but I want to try and make it as good as we can for Emelia."

"Agreed. I don't know how, but we can try." I shrugged and smiled. "We'll think of somethin'. Can I get a closer look at the horses?" Gazing up at Wyatt with hopeful eyes, I placed my hands in a praying position just below my chin.

He chuckled. "Of course."

We walked side by side to where the horses stood in the middle of the corral, grazing on grass. With my five-foot-four frame, Wyatt matched my two steps with one of his own. He was about four inches taller than me, and it seemed as if it was all in his legs.

"Hey, Minnie," I greeted the mare. I kept my voice soft and low so I didn't startle her or Flash. I slowly lifted my hand to the side of her face. I whispered to her, "You're a gorgeous girl." As I studied Minnie, I forgot anyone else—even time—existed. There was only one other being that made me feel that way.

Minnie stood still. Her head turned slightly and looked in my direction. Her tail whipped back and forth. She allowed me to run my hands along her side. Her coat was rough in a few places, probably from not being groomed for so long. In other places, it was as smooth as silk.

In a matter of minutes, though, Flash took off—well, like a flash—to the other side of the corral, and Minnie ran after him. *Definitely bonded to each other.* But I guess that would be anyone when all they had was each other.

I lifted my eyes up to Wyatt. It must have been hard being a kid and having no one. I was so glad Uncle Colt found him. My heart began to speed up, and my palms started to sweat. I needed to tell him how I felt about him, but I just couldn't. One, I didn't want to lose my best friend. And two, he deserved someone who was healthy. But my heart ached every time I thought of him with someone else.

"Well, I guess we know why he's called Flash." I giggled softly.

Wyatt smiled that smile again. The one that gave my heart a flutter. "Yeah."

I sighed.

"What's wrong?" He said, turning to me.

My eyes grew as I realized I'd sighed out loud. "Nothin's

wrong. Just so happy to be home. It's funny, though. I couldn't wait to leave, and then, when I did, I couldn't wait to come home. I missed everyone so much."

"Even me?" he asked.

"*Especially* you." My cheeks grew warm at the admission.

The smile that spread across Wyatt's face told me he was more than satisfied with my answer. He pointed his thumb over his shoulder in the direction of the house. "It's almost time for supper. Do ya wanna join us? I'm sure no one would object to seein' ya."

"Um. Sure. Why not?" I shrugged. "I just need to get my kit from my car."

"Okay. I'll walk with ya." He extended his arm for me to walk first.

As we made our way through the stable, it was quiet as Aunt Callie had already cleaned up and left.

"Hi, Warrior," I greeted him as we passed by his stall.

Warrior raised his head and snorted his own greeting in response.

My car was only a few short steps from the stable door. Wyatt opened the passenger side door for me like the gentleman he was. I grabbed my kit from the seat.

"Do you mind if I do this here so I can leave my kit?"

"Sure. Do ya need me to do anythin'?"

Wyatt had seen me take my insulin so many times over the years, but every single time, he asked if there was anything I needed. He was sweet that way.

"Actually, I guess I should see what we're havin' first so I know how much to take." I rolled my eyes at myself.

Spontaneous dinner nights were one reason I hated the disease. I couldn't just sit down and enjoy a meal. First, I had to calculate the number of carbs I'd be eating and then inject enough insulin to break those carbs down. And of course, there was the fifteen-minute wait in between. Granted, I had the monitor on my arm, but it was still so new to me that I didn't trust it completely. So, I just continued doing things the way I always had.

I just wanted to be normal. I never questioned why God chose me for the disease, though. I trusted He had a plan.

"I've missed havin' ya 'round," Wyatt confessed as we stepped onto the porch of the main house.

"I've missed bein' here. Wish Quinn was still here." The realization that she wouldn't be in the kitchen to greet me hit harder than I thought as tears pricked my eyes. *Will all the firsts be this hard?*

"Yeah. It's been . . . different." Wyatt opened the door and swept his hand in front of him. "After you."

"Thank you." I smiled.

The kitchen was alive with chatter. Just like it always was.

"Caitlyn!" Uncle Colt shouted above all the noise as he extended his arms wide.

Immediately, the room became deafeningly quiet, and all eyes focused on me. Heat rose to my cheeks.

"Hey, Uncle Colt!" I ran into his arms, wrapping my own around his waist. I glanced up at him. *Should I tell him in front of everyone?* "Can I talk to you about somethin'?"

He nodded.

I looked around at the others as I stepped away from his embrace, twisting my hands in front of me. "Promise you won't get mad?"

He placed his hands on his waist. "Well, now, when you start it out like that . . ."

"I wanted to tell you . . . well, everyone really, that I'm not going back to school." I winced as the final word passed my lips.

"What?" Uncle Colt's voice boomed. "What do you mean? Do Marci and Chuck know about this?"

"Yes. I told them earlier today." I grinned nervously. "I want to be an EMT and eventually a paramedic. For certain reasons." My gaze fell to Emelia.

"And what reasons might those be?" Uncle Colt stood with his feet shoulder-width apart and his arms crossed over his chest, his jaw tightly clenched.

"Um." My eyes bounced from him back to Emelia as the tears welled up in my eyes. "I feel like if I'd been trained and been at the fair that night . . ."

"Oh, Caitlyn." Emelia stood from the table and rushed around it to engulf me in a hug. She whispered in my ear, "There wasn't anything anyone could have done to save her." Then, she retreated from the hug and said barely loud enough for me to hear, "Except for me."

Never in my life did I think three little words could break my heart the way those words ripped through it.

"But it made me realize that I want to be a first responder and help people in the middle of their emergency, not after. I've spent a lot of time in prayer about it, and I believe God is leading me in this direction."

"Are your parents okay with this?" Aunt Callie asked in a much more loving tone than Uncle Colt.

"I don't really know for sure. They just said if it's from God, the door will be open. And if it's what will make me happy." I shrugged.

"Well, it'll be good to have you home then," Uncle Colt said before wrapping me in another hug.

I sighed with relief as I squeezed his middle. This time, though, I breathed in deep and held on a little tighter. A little longer.

After leaving my uncle's arms, I turned toward the older man standing by the stove. "Richard, can I see what we're havin' so I can take my insulin?"

"Sure." He smiled and motioned toward the counter where a piece of paper sat.

"What's this?" I asked, pointing to it.

"When Callie said you were here, I took down the carbohydrates that were in each item as I made them. Just in case you decided to stay for supper." He winked with a smile.

"You didn't have to do that." A tear threatened my eye. "But I appreciate you so much."

I wrapped my arms around him. Richard had been a staple at the ranch ever since I could remember. I considered him like a grandparent. I had become seasoned at counting carbs, but it was nice to have it already calculated for me. Especially with the aroma of chicken, roasted potatoes, and green beans filling the air and making my mouth water.

I did my best to sidestep out of the kitchen to the hallway bathroom without being noticed. I took out my insulin pen and twisted the dial to the amount of medicine I needed. I took in a breath before putting it to my stomach and pressing the button. That was so much easier than a few years before, when I had to use a bigger needle and a bottle of insulin. It had been so hard to do when I first started. Sticking a needle in my stomach, that is. I still hated it, but I didn't hesitate anymore. It definitely hurt worse when I hesitated.

When I returned to the kitchen, everyone else welcomed me home with pats on the back, hugs, and "welcome home."

Finally, the commotion died down, and we sat at the dinner table. Richard set the dishes of food in the center of the long wooden table. The table, like Richard, was a staple in the Andrews' house. It was older than I was. Maybe even older than Uncle Colt. It stood the test of time, that was for sure.

The aroma of the food hit my nose once more, knocking me out of my memories. Oh, how I'd missed Richard's cooking. I inhaled, closing my eyes and breathing in the scents of the different foods, allowing the smells to fully invade my nostrils. Everything smelled so delicious. It was hard not to dig in immediately.

"Let's say grace." Uncle Colt took hold of Aunt Callie's hand and Emelia's on his other side.

I watched as Emelia joined hands with Luke and Luke with Spencer. Richard was at the other end of the table. He held hands with Spencer and Wyatt. Austin used to sit in that seat. Wyatt held my hand, and warmth radiated up my arm. I held Aunt Callie's hand to complete the circle.

"Father, God, we come together tonight to give thanks for all the gifts You have given us on this fine day," Uncle Colt began. "The friendships. The family. This delicious food. We ask that You use this food to nourish our bodies so we can continue to do Your will. We praise You. We thank You. We love You. Forever. In Christ's mighty name. Amen."

Amens followed all around the table.

As we began passing around the food, I took in the sight of the people seated there. I'd known some of them for what felt like forever—some of them my whole life. A smile crept to my lips. These people were my extended family.

When my eyes landed on Emelia, I could see the ghost of who she'd been just a few months before. Luke sat next to her, no doubt holding her hand under the table as they both ate with one hand. I prayed every chance I got that God would restore her soul and breathe new life into her. I closed my eyes and sent those thoughts up to Him.

Seeing the love between Emelia and Luke and Uncle Colt

and Aunt Callie made my heart ache for the same in my own life. Maybe one day soon, I'd tell Wyatt exactly how I felt. I was terrified of losing him, but I was also terrified he'd feel the same way. Because if he felt the same way, how could I ask him to deal with my diabetes and the challenges it had?

Do not fear, Daughter. Cast your burden on Me, and I will sustain you.

Thank you, Lord. I know in Your time I will have the courage to give him my entire heart.

"Hey." Wyatt bumped my right arm and brought me back to the kitchen table. He leaned over and whispered, "You okay?"

I smiled and met his eyes. "Yeah. Just enjoyin' the fullness of this room."

"How come ya didn't tell me you were leavin' school?" Hurt radiated from his voice.

I laid my hand on his arm. "I'm sorry. I should've told you. I wanted to tell my mom and dad first. I didn't realize I would be telling Uncle Colt and Aunt Callie in front of everyone."

"It's okay. I'm just glad you're goin' to be home again." He patted my hand.

I returned my attention to my plate, my hand buzzing from the jolt of electricity at Wyatt's contact with my hand. Listening to the chatter all around me, Quinn drifted through my mind. An ache formed in my heart. She would have undoubtedly been the center of attention, dancing around the table, making everyone laugh and spreading so much sunshine. Her arms spread out to her sides, her dress billowing, her long blonde curls bouncing off her shoulders, and her pink cowgirl boots tapping on the floor as she twirled around.

A tear appeared at the corner of my eye, but it lingered on my eyelashes. That little girl had only been in my life for a few months, but she left an imprint on my heart that would last my lifetime. Life in Edenton was going to be different without her in it.

When my plate was being removed from in front of me, my mind returned to the present. I gazed up to find Aunt Callie staring down at me. My cheeks grew warm, and a sheepish grin appeared on my lips. "Sorry."

"Lost in your thoughts?"

"Yeah. Thinkin' 'bout Quinn and where to start now that I'm back home."

"I can understand that. Everything will work out the way God intends it to." She smiled and squeezed my shoulder before taking the stack of dishes she had tucked in her other arm over to the sink.

I wished I could stay at the ranch forever. I loved it there. But as I peeked at my watch, I realized I needed to get home. I moseyed over to the sink. "It was so good to see you, Aunt Callie."

"Leaving so soon?" She dried her hands on a red and white checkered towel.

"Yeah. I'd better get home." I smiled as I wrapped an arm around her back.

"Well, don't be a stranger."

"I won't. I promise."

I strode out the door and plowed right into something solid, yet a little squishy. "Oof." I tried my best to keep my balance.

Arms came around me. "Easy there. You okay, Chipmunk?"

I lifted my face and found Wyatt's lips a whisper away from mine. Oh, how I wanted him to kiss me. I shook my head. *What? No! Boundaries, Caitlyn!*

"No? You're not okay? What's wrong?" Panic filled his voice.

"I'm fine." I pushed myself off his chest and tugged at my shirt to straighten it. My mouth was suddenly as dry as the sand in the Sahara. Not that I'd ever been there to know, though. *Space. I need space.* "I'll see you soon, Wyatt."

I jumped from the porch and hurriedly went to my car. I didn't take a breath until I was seated inside with the door closed. And locked.

Chapter 3

Wyatt

That was close! I almost kissed her. Wait. When we were alone, she only called me by my name when she was nervous about something. My brows furrowed in confusion. I sighed and rolled my eyes. *I can't let that happen again. I can't lose my best friend bein' stupid and kissin' her.* I shook my head as I opened the door to the kitchen.

I had originally gone back to the house to say goodnight to Caitlyn. But since I was already outside the door, I figured I'd go inside and say goodnight to whoever was still there. When I stepped inside, Callie was the only one present, still cleaning up from supper.

"Just wanted to say goodnight, Callie."

"Oh, goodnight, Wyatt." She turned from where she was wiping down the table and smiled. "See you in the morning."

I tipped my hat before retreating out the door.

As I stepped inside my cabin, I grabbed my phone from my pocket. I scrolled to Caitlyn's number and typed out a message.

> *Hey, I forgot to ask you. Do you want to go to the Kickoff to Christmas with me tomorrow?*

I hit the arrow to send the message and waited. My breath

stuck in my throat. I didn't know why I was so nervous. We'd gone together every year, but I'd never asked before. It just usually came up in conversation. *Ooh. Three dots.*

Of course, silly. We always go together :)

Good night and sweet dreams, Chipmunk.

Good night and sweet dreams, Cowboy.

Maybe I should just blurt out how I feel about her, I thought. *God, help me. I don't know what to do.* I sat down on my couch, leaned my head back, and closed my eyes.
Rest in Me and wait patiently.
I smiled as the darkness of sleep washed over me.

* * *

The next morning, I woke up with excitement coursing through my veins. The Kickoff to Christmas Festival was one of my favorite festivals of the whole year. And not just because I got to experience it with Caitlyn. That was the cherry on top. I hurriedly changed my clothes and scurried out to get my chores done. The festival started at four.

As I stepped through the open doorway of the stable, my eyes took a minute to adjust to the dim light of the yellow bulbs hanging from the ceiling beams. Warrior raised and lowered his head in greeting, just like he did whenever anyone came into the stable. The scent of hay mixed with manure hit me. *Guess I know what my job is today.* I noticed Luke and Majesty in front of Majesty's stall.

"Hey, Luke," I greeted him.

"Oh, hey, Wyatt. How are ya?" He tightened the strap on Majesty's saddle.

"I'm good. And you?"

"Not too bad. Gettin' ready to head out to check the fence and make sure things are good out in the pasture. We've heard some rumblin's about coyotes. Don't need 'em gettin' too close, ya know?"

"Yeah. That wouldn't be good. How's Emelia doin'?"

"As good as can be expected, I suppose. Christmas is gonna hit her hard, I'm sure. I'm hopin' to convince her to come to the festival tonight. But not sure I'll have much luck." Luke shrugged before climbing into the saddle.

"Caitlyn and I are tryin' to plan somethin' special for her for Christmas, but not sure what yet."

"Thanks, Wyatt. I'm sure she'll love whatever ya come up with."

"Have a safe ride." I raised my hand in a wave.

"Thanks." Luke clucked his tongue and nudged Majesty into motion.

Emelia wasn't the only one who changed with the death of Quinn. Luke didn't act like the same man. He didn't smile quite as often, and when he did, it never reached his eyes. My hope was that they both would get the spark for life back. Eventually.

I grabbed the nearby rake and began mucking out the stalls. That was everyone's least favorite chore, but it had to be done by *someone*. That someone was usually me. Luckily, the bedding didn't need to be changed. I hoped anyway.

"Hey, Warrior." I reached out my hand to caress the side of his face. "Time to get some exercise while I clean out your stall. Would ya like that, buddy?"

I lifted the lead rope from the hook next to his stall. Sticking a sugar cube under his nose, I slipped the rope over his head and then led him out to the corral. I didn't really have to use the sugar cube, but I knew the horses liked them, so I gave the cubes to them anyway.

It amazed me how far Warrior had come since he arrived at the ranch, battered and scared of everything and everyone. Except Callie. But, then again, *everyone* loved Callie.

I sauntered back to the stable. It was one of my favorite places to be. Surrounded by horses. Horses didn't belittle you or care what your weight or age was. They didn't care if you were beautiful or ugly—on the outside, anyway. They didn't care what your political views were and didn't care if you felt like you should've been better owners or caretakers. Horses were always excited to see you and be close to you. They love you without limits.

Too bad people aren't more like horses. All animals, really.

When I was done with Warrior's stall, I retrieved him from the corral and repeated those steps with the remaining seven horses. Horses were my favorite part of ranch life. Each horse had its own personality. The horses allowed me to take the time to talk about my feelings. I didn't feel safe talking about them to any human. Except maybe Colt, but I hadn't confided in him about Caitlyn. Only the horses and God knew my true feelings.

As I was putting Flash back in his stall, he pinched the top of my hat between his teeth.

"Hey, now, boy." I turned and retrieved my hat from his lips.

Flash's head bounced up and down as he neighed. It was like he was laughing at me. I shook my head and chuckled as I plopped my hat back on my head.

My stomach growled, and I headed to the house for lunch. In my excitement for the festival, I'd immediately set out to do chores and completely forgot to eat breakfast.

The kitchen was alive, just as it always was at any given

mealtime. I surveyed the room and smiled. My eyes stopped at each person, and I gave thanks to God for this chosen family. If it weren't for them and my faith in God, who knows where I would have ended up. Jail or dead would've been my guess. I washed my hands in the kitchen sink before taking my seat at the table.

After Colt prayed over the food, I took a cue from Caitlyn and embraced the opportunity to just enjoy the company around the old kitchen table. First, there was Colt. The man who took a chance on a homeless teenager and took me in when I had nowhere else to go. He was more of a dad to me than my own had ever been. He taught me everything he knew about ranch life—life in general, really. He had been through a lot in his own life—the death of his father, abandonment by the woman he thought he would spend the rest of his life with—but God had other plans for him. The abandonment he felt shaped him into a man who would do everything in his power to never abandon anyone, human or animal. For that, I was so grateful.

Sitting next to Colt was Callie. She was like the mother I had always wanted but wasn't blessed to have. Her arrival at Redemption Ranch made everything better. She had been through so much loss and pain in her own life, including he death of her parents on her sixteenth birthday and abuse at the hands of her aunt that left scars, not only on her body but on her heart. Even so, Callie gave her heart to Colt and this ranch. She managed to make Colt a better man somehow. I hadn't even known that was possible.

Emelia sat on the other side of Colt. Her existence at the ranch had been short but impactful, especially after the loss of Quinn. She had dealt with the loss with such grace that I knew could only come from God. Emelia and Quinn were two of the most kind and loving people I'd ever met. She had her own demons from which she was still reeling. All in God's time.

Next was Luke. He was like a big brother to me. He had fought things as a United States Marine that I could never imagine. He was a lot like Warrior, battered and scarred. On the inside *and* the outside. But he never complained. He was one of the hardest workers I'd ever seen. When Colt hadn't had time to teach me about hard work, Luke had stepped in.

Jon was like the fun uncle. He always had a joke or knew how to make you laugh when you needed it the most. I think that stemmed from his losing his wife at a young age. He never got the chance to grow old with her, the woman who held his heart. He hadn't allowed another woman in since. At least not that I had seen. I wasn't as close with him, but I knew I could count on him for anything I needed at any time.

Spencer was like a brother, also. He was closest to me in age. He had come to the ranch after losing everything in Montana. He knew the meaning of hard work and set out to be the best version of himself that he could be. Over the last year, he had really put in hard work on himself. On the inside as well as the outside. We had spent time talking about the Bible and God together. He also had been working out and had packed on some muscle. *I could afford to do that, too. Maybe shed a few pounds in the process.*

I was appreciative of every person around the table. Especially the people they had become in spite of what they'd been through. A grin washed over my face. Yes, life at the ranch was the best. The only life I wanted. Besides a life with Caitlyn, that is.

I lifted the burger from my plate and took a bite as I listened to everyone's conversations around me. There was absolutely nothing like family, even if they weren't my family by blood.

As everyone was finishing up their lunch, Colt stood at the head of the table. "Okay. Let's clean up and get the rest of our chores done so we can all head to the festival," he said.

Chair legs scraping across the floor rang out in the kitchen as everyone began to chatter about the festival. Everyone except for Emelia and Luke.

After leaving the house, I checked on the horses I'd left in the corral, Minnie and Flash.

"Hey, Flash." I stroked the side of his face. "How are ya, boy?"

Flash snickered in response.

"Wanna go for a ride?"

Minnie joined us as soon as the question left my mouth.

"Hey, Minnie. You wanna go for a ride, too? Good idea. I'll call Chipmunk and see if she wants to join us." A smile spread across my lips.

Any time I got to spend with Caitlyn was a good time. No! A wonderful time. We could take a short ride and then head to the festival. I led Flash and Minnie back to the stable and then dialed her number.

"Hey, Cowboy. I wasn't expectin' to hear from ya till later."

"I wanted to see if ya wanted to take a ride with me, Flash, and Minnie. It's been a bit since they've had a good run."

"Sure." Caitlyn's smile could be heard in her voice.

"I'll get them ready, then. See ya soon."

"See ya soon."

I slid my phone into my back pocket. "Flash, you and Minnie ready to go for a ride?"

I began to tack up the horses while I waited for Caitlyn to arrive. It wasn't long before her car skidded to a stop in the gravel outside the stable. I peered through the half-open door as she stood from the driver's seat. She had her blonde hair pulled up in a ponytail on top of her head. She looked so good in her brown boots and worn blue jeans. Well, the boots and jeans didn't have anything to do with it, really. She always looked good. In my eyes, anyway.

Lord have mercy. "Ya ready?" I asked as I guided the horses out of the stable and held out Minnie's reins to Caitlyn.

"Absolutely." She grabbed the reins and boosted herself into the saddle. I did the same with Flash.

We walked the horses for a little while before Caitlyn called out, "Race ya!" She and Minnie sprinted off.

"Oh, Flash, we can't let the girls win!" I clicked my heels against his sides, and we took off.

Caitlyn's laughter floated through the air. It was the most beautiful sound I'd ever heard. Like an angel's song. It was something I could handle hearing every day for the rest of my life, and it'd never be enough.

When Flash and I finally caught up to them and slowed down, Caitlyn's face was flushed from the wind, her laughter still pouring from her lips. "We won! We won!" she said, raising her arms in victory.

I laughed. "Yes. Yes, you did, but only because you cheated."

"We did *not* cheat, did we, Minnie?" She patted the horse on the neck.

"We'll let you have the win. *This* time." *Every time.*

We stared out at the expanse that was before us. The land was always so beautiful, even in winter. I couldn't believe I got to live there every day. The trees rocked back and forth in the slight breeze. Different colored flowers decorated various places in the field.

The horses lowered their heads to graze on the grass as we

took a break.

"It's so beautiful here. Why did I ever want to leave?" Caitlyn said softly.

I knew it was a question she didn't want answered, so I let it fade into the wind. "Wanna head back so we can get ready for the festival?" I tilted my head to focus my attention on her.

"Yeah." Her lips widened into a pearly white smile. "I can't wait."

We let the horses walk back to the stable to give them time to cool down from their sprint. I wanted this time to last forever. I always did. But I was excited to spend the evening at the festival with Caitlyn. She loved it just as much as I did.

When we got back to the stable, we both jumped down off the horses and loosened the cinch on each saddle around the belly of the horses.

"You can go ahead and go, Caitlyn, so you can get ready if ya want to."

"No. I want to help. It's part of the responsibility of ridin', right? Make sure the horse is taken care of after the ride? Isn't that what Uncle Colt always says?"

I smiled. "That's true. He *does* always say that."

We removed the tack from each horse and walked them over to a nearby water barrel. I used this time to observe how each horse was walking and their general attitude. Neither of them was limping nor appeared to be in any discomfort. They both seemed to have enjoyed the ride.

"Let's go ahead and turn them out," I said. "I'll put them in their stalls when I get back from the festival, but let's check their feet for anythin' first."

After we lifted each leg and inspected the horses' shoes to make sure they were on securely and that nothing was in their hooves, we took them to the corral. It seemed to be the place where the two horses were happiest. Because they were together. Made me think of Caitlyn and me.

"So, I'll meet ya at your house? Say 4:30?" I suggested.

"Sounds good. See ya then."

"See ya."

Caitlyn disappeared into her car and drove down the dirt road toward the main gate, and I jogged up to my cabin to shower and get ready.

"What am I gonna wear?" I asked out loud, standing in front of my closet. I blew out a breath as I scratched the back of my head.

I slid each hanger across the bar that held my shirts in place, eyeing each and every one. When I came across my emerald-green, button-down, long-sleeve, flannel shirt, I slipped it from its hanger. I didn't normally care what I wore; I'd simply grab a shirt and put it on. But this was Caitlyn. I always tried to look my best for her. As best I could, anyway. She always liked that shirt. She said it made the green in my eyes pop. Whatever that meant. My eyes were blue, but every once in a while, the green would come through.

As I stood in front of the bathroom mirror, I ran my hand over the five o'clock shadow that had made its appearance well before five o'clock. I grabbed my shaving cream and razor from the medicine cabinet and lathered my face before putting the razor to the stubble.

I slathered on some aftershave—Caitlyn's favorite, of course—and headed back into my room to retrieve my shirt, clean black jeans, and clean black boots. They weren't as worn as my favorite everyday boots, but they were almost as comfortable.

Grabbing my keys from the top of the old wooden dresser Colt had given me—the first dresser I ever had—I strode to the door. I plopped my brown leather cowboy hat on top of my head, slid on my jean jacket, and sauntered out the door.

It wasn't long before I pulled up to the curb in front of Caitlyn's house. I breathed deeply. I wiped my clammy hands down the length of my thighs.

Why am I so nervous? It's just Chipmunk. I knew before the thought entered my head that it wasn't *just* Chipmunk. I knew in my heart, 100 percent, without a doubt, she was my person. Somehow, I needed to get up the courage to tell her. *One day. Maybe.* Soon.

I rapped my knuckles on the white front door of the dark teal house. When I heard the doorknob twist, I plastered on my best grin, hoping it looked more genuine than it felt.

"Hey, Wyatt!" Mrs. Logan greeted me with her usual warm smile and welcoming spirit.

The Logans were the type of family that if I had to put together a picture of the perfect family for me, they would be it. They were just good, honest, comforting people.

"Hi, Mrs. Logan. How are ya?" I lifted my hat off my head.

"I'm great. Excited for the festivities." She closed the door behind me.

"Me, too. Is Chip— Caitlyn ready?" A sheepish grin formed on my lips.

Mrs. Logan's brows furrowed as heat rose to my cheeks. *Yep. She noticed my almost slip-up.*

"I'll go check."

She left me standing by the front door as she peered up the staircase before disappearing down the hallway.

"Hey, Wyatt!" Caitlyn appeared in the middle of the staircase.

My breath hitched in my throat. Her sparkling red sweater

was a good contrast to her fair skin and long blonde hair. She had on blue jeans and a pair of knee-high black boots. She never wore too much makeup, which suited me just fine. She had enough on to make her blue eyes shine.

I, once again, dragged my palms down my thighs. "Wow. You. Look. Amazin'."

"Thank you." She smiled as she tucked her hair behind her ear. "You don't look so bad yourself." Her smile brightened up her whole face.

"Ya ready ta go?"

"Yep. See ya later, Mom!"

I opened the door and allowed Caitlyn to walk ahead of me.

"Always the gentleman," she said, laying her hand over her heart.

"Of course. Always for my lady." I gulped. *Did I just say that out loud?* My eyes almost bulged out of my head. *Maybe she didn't notice.*

I took a chance and peeked at her. Her brow raised ever-so-slightly. The air from my lungs caught in my throat. *She noticed.* When she didn't say anything, I exhaled.

"Do ya wanna walk?" she asked.

"Sure." *Anything to spend more time with you.*

I held my right elbow out so Caitlyn could hold on to it as we made our way down the road to the bay where the festival was already underway. Her heels clicked as they hit the concrete sidewalk. I never got tired of walking in her neighborhood. Most of the homes were large Victorian houses mixed with some Tudor-style ones and other smaller types. I knew the first time I headed down Broad Street that it was the old part of town.

As we strolled further down the street, we passed by the

Edenton Inn on the opposite side of us. Carl and Marie, Colt's aunt and uncle, were the owners. They had been talking about retiring and moving to Florida, where Colt's mom had moved a few years before. I hoped that if they sold the inn, the new owners would love the place as much as Carl and Marie did.

On the corner was the church we attended, Lighthouse Community Church. I loved the look of the white brick building with the tall steeple.

Broad Street ended at the bay. It was my favorite part of town. More often than not, it was quiet and peaceful. But today, it was bustling with kids' laughter and people's chatter. Food trucks were scattered about. I could smell the sweet scent of kettle corn and the spicy aroma of Italian sausage. Country music blasted through the air from a stage in the parking lot of the welcome center.

"Do ya wanna go up on the lighthouse deck?" Caitlyn asked as she twirled to face me and took a couple of steps backward toward the lighthouse.

"Sure, Chipmunk." I enjoyed the shade of pink her face turned every time I called her by her nickname.

We strode up the ramp to the first level of the lighthouse. Someone had twisted white string lights around the railing up the ramp and along the deck. The water lapped against the legs of the lighthouse platform.

Caitlyn sat down on the wood deck and lay her arms on the lower part of the railing. She sighed. "This is my most favorite place ever. Besides the ranch, of course," she confessed. "I come here a lot to think and figure things out."

I thought I knew everything about her. But that I hadn't known. I stared out over the water at the city, barely visible from our perch. "I can see why. I love coming to the water, too. Somethin' 'bout the silence and the water lapping the shoreline. Gives you a closeness to God that is hard to describe."

"Agreed."

We sat in silence for what seemed like forever, but any moments I got to steal with her were worth everything to me.

"Ready to see what's happenin'?" Caitlyn asked, breaking the quietness.

"Of course."

We stood and strolled down the ramp, the spell of being alone with her broken as soon as we stepped onto the grass at the end of the ramp.

"Are ya hungry?" I glanced over at her.

"Aren't I always?" She giggled.

"Did ya take your insulin?"

"I did. Right before I met ya at the door. But I brought my meter and insulin pen." She patted the bag hanging at her side.

I nodded in satisfaction. I knew she was perfectly capable of handling her diabetes all on her own, but I wanted to protect her and make sure she knew she was cared about. It was the most important thing to me.

"What are ya in the mood for?" I asked.

She pulled her bottom lip between her teeth. Then, she twirled around in a circle, taking in all of the food trucks. "How about street tacos?"

"Street tacos it is, then."

With food in hand, we sat at the picnic table at the edge of the water, tucked between two trees.

"Mmmm." She closed her eyes as she slowly chewed her food, savoring the bite.

"Good?" I chuckled. "You have somethin' . . ." I motioned to the side of her mouth.

Her eyes grew wide. "What? Where?" She wiped the opposite side of her face.

"Here, let me." I took my thumb and wiped the corner of her mouth. My thumb moved in slow motion. Time stood still as I stared at my thumb moving along the side of her mouth. I coughed to clear my throat and whispered, "Um. There. I got it."

Caitlyn's cheeks became rosy. "Thank you." She peeked at her watch. "It's almost time for the tree lighting. It's my favorite part. Besides the Flotilla boat parade, of course."

"Of course." I couldn't seem to take my eyes off her.

We threw our trash in the nearby trash can before finding a good spot to watch the tree lighting.

"Okay, everyone!" Mayor Travers spoke into the microphone on the platform next to the tree. "We're ready to light up the tree. Thank you to Earthy Expressions for donating the tree again this year . . ."

"Did you remember to bring an ornament?" I leaned into Caitlyn's ear. Her strawberry shampoo tickled my nose. It was my favorite.

"Of course." She pulled something out of her bag and hid it between her palms. Her eyes locked on mine. "Did you?"

"Of course." I held up my index finger where a light brown horse that I had made earlier in the year dangled from a silver string. I had painted "Tinkerbell" in pink along the side of the horse. In honor of Quinn.

"Did you make that?" Caitlyn smiled as she held it in her fingertips. "I love it."

"Yep. Do I get to see yours?" I tried to peek into her hands.

"Not yet." She pulled her hands closer to her body.

"Okay. On the count of three!" Mayor Travers held up his hand.

"One! Two! Three!" the crowd shouted out.

Mayor Travers pushed the button, and the lights began to

light up the tree. Gasps rang out among the onlookers. "Now, as is tradition," the mayor continued, "you may place your ornaments on the tree. For those who are new to this, every year, we place new ornaments on the tree. This has been a tradition dating back to the first Edenton Christmas in 1722. You can feel free to browse the Welcome Center, where they have on display the different ornaments that have adorned the tree since the 1700s. Thank you all for coming out to celebrate our kickoff to the Christmas season. The Flotilla will start in about an hour." Mayor Travers set down the microphone and hopped off the platform.

It was one of the most beautiful trees I'd ever seen. Of course, I said that every year. It was always a tree that was so full and green with different colored lights from the bottom to the top. It wasn't ever too tall of a tree so that when people placed their ornaments on it, there would be some at the top and not just at the bottom. It was always a treat to see the ornaments people left on the tree.

I gazed over at Caitlyn. Her eyes were glued to the lights like a moth to a flame. Her smile was so big and wide that her teeth glistened in the light.

Caitlyn sighed. "That's my favorite part."

I wanted to tell her that *my* favorite part was spending the time with her. Instead, I said, "Mine, too. Do you want to put the ornaments on the tree now or later?" I really wanted to see her ornament.

"Now."

We made our way up to the tree through the crowd. I placed my ornament in the middle. I closed my eyes and sent a message up to heaven. *For you, Quinn.* "Where do you want to put yours?"

"Um." Caitlyn sucked her bottom lip into her mouth. "I

think right here." She raised up on her tiptoes and wrapped the light-pink ribbon around the branch.

When she let go, I finally caught a glimpse of what she had been holding. It was a silver ornament in the shape of a little girl with angel wings dancing. Engraved on the bottom of it were the words *Dancing in the sky with the angels*. It had Quinn's name etched into it with the dates of her life.

We both dedicated our ornaments to Quinn. Ornaments that will keep her memory alive for as long as the tradition stands. I swiped at a tear and whispered, "Oh, that's the perfect ornament."

I wrapped my arm around Caitlyn's shoulders and pulled her to me. When her arms came around me, warmth radiated through my entire body.

"I don't know about that. You made yours, and it's for Quinn, too. That makes it pretty perfect also."

I squeezed her tighter. Closer.

"Okay, folks. The Flotilla is about to start. Head on over to the water." Mayor Travers's voice rang out into the night air.

"Do you want to get a hot chocolate first?" I asked Caitlyn. "It's a little colder this year than usual."

She shivered. "Yes, please."

I slid my arms from my jacket and wrapped it around her shoulders as we stood in line at the hot chocolate cart. Once we had hot chocolate in hand, we strode over to find a spot to watch the Flotilla.

The Flotilla seemed odd the first time I came to the festival. I had seen regular parades for Christmas but never a parade of boats. It was awesome. All the boats were decked out in Christmas lights. One even had Christmas music that caused some of the spectators to break out in dance moves. Oohs and aahs filled the air by the kids as each boat appeared in front of them. I always loved seeing this parade through the eyes of the kids. *I wish Quinn was one of those kids.*

After the last boat disappeared around the corner of the bay, a screech sounded over the loudspeaker. "Sorry about that," Mayor Travers spoke into the microphone once again. "The boats were exceptional this year, weren't they?" He said *that* every year, too. Laughter floated around us. "Are y'all ready to dance?"

"Yeah!" kids from all over the street screamed.

"Are we going to stay for the dance?" Caitlyn asked with hope-filled eyes.

How can I refuse those eyes? "You and I both know I can't dance a lick."

"Can't or won't?" She giggled.

"Can't *and* won't." I attempted to stand my ground.

Music started blaring just up the street from where we stood. Caitlyn grabbed my hand and tried to pull me up the street. My feet were planted firmly in place. "Come on. Please?"

Those eyes. I groaned. "Ugh. Fine."

She hadn't let go of my hand. Heat began to seep up my arm as she pulled me along until we were smack dab in the middle of the dance area. She grabbed my other hand and started moving my arms with hers. "Come on," she begged.

My head fell back in a groan, and I rolled my eyes but could not stop a laugh from escaping. I did my best to move my feet with the music. I felt like an idiot. A real beauty and the beast moment.

A slow song started, and couples filled the dance floor, leaving me trapped. Someone bumped into me, pushing me closer to Caitlyn. "Dance with me," she spoke softly. She pulled me closer and wrapped her arms around my neck.

I slid my arms around her waist and swayed as best as I could to the music. *Please don't step on her toes. Please don't step on her toes.*

I loved having the girl of my dreams in my arms. It felt right. It felt like home. I opened my mouth to tell her my feelings, but the song ended. I exhaled sharply. I didn't like that her arms left my body as it sent a cold chill down my spine.

The sound of little kids' laughter echoed in my ears just before Caitlyn was surrounded by a group of giggling girls. "Caitlyn!" a couple of them yelled.

Caitlyn's laugh floated to my ears. I'd never get tired of her laugh. Her laugh made my lips turn up into a smile.

"Hey, girls!" she greeted them as she wrapped her arms around the group.

"We've missed you!" little Emma exclaimed.

"Oh, I've missed you all, too. So much! Have you all kept dancing?"

"Yes!" they all exclaimed at one time.

"Good!"

"Are you gonna come back?" Lainey asked.

"I'm going to ask if I can."

"Yay!" They all jumped up and down.

"I'll see you later, girls. Okay?"

"Bye, Caitlyn!" They waved before running away, giggling.

"Sorry about that." Caitlyn twirled around and faced me again.

"No worries," I said as I glanced up at the twinkling lights against the darkness of the sky. "Can I walk you home?"

"I'd love that." She twisted her hands in front of her, her cheeks turning a light shade of pink.

I lifted my elbow, and she looped her arm through mine. Heat once again ran up my arm and straight to my heart. We traipsed up the street in silence. The streetlights lit a path down the sidewalk and street.

"I had a really good time tonight." Caitlyn slid her hand into mine and squeezed as her voice danced in the night air. "Thank you."

My heart pounded against my ribs, threatening to burst. "I did, too."

She rested her head on my arm for a few steps. It was nice. It was more than nice, really. I loved the comfort of our relationship, even though I wanted more. I just wasn't sure she wanted the same. I was scared to ask. Scared to admit I'd let her all the way into my heart. Would she leave just like my parents did?

The Logan house came into view much too soon. Our time together was never long enough. All the time in the world would never be long enough. Not for Caitlyn. A sigh escaped my lips.

"What's wrong?" She peered up at me.

"Nothin'. Just not ready to go home yet."

"Yeah. Me neither, but I guess we have to at some point, right?" Caitlyn placed her hand on my forearm and gently squeezed. I was sure the heat from her hand would leave a burn mark.

We stood at the door. *Just say it, Wyatt. Just blurt it out that you are in love with her.* I sucked in a deep breath. "Chipmunk, I—"

The front door flew open, cutting off my declaration. *No!*

"Caitlyn! Sis!" Dyl appeared with his arms stretched out. "I thought we were gonna hang out at the festival."

"Sorry, Dyl." The light in Caitlyn's eyes dimmed.

"I'm just teasin' ya. I knew you were with Wyatt. When are you guys gonna date already?"

"Dyl!" Caitlyn's cheeks flushed a deep red this time.

I was sure my face matched hers.

Dyl shrugged and went back inside.

"I'm sorry about him." Caitlyn pointed her thumb over her shoulder.

"No need to be. I should be goin'. Have a great night, Chipmunk." I leaned down and kissed her cheek.

"Oh. Here's your jacket back. Thank you." She slipped her arms out of it and held it out.

"Thanks." I took it and made a beeline for my truck. As much as I had wanted to tell her the truth about my feelings, I was halfway relieved Dyl had interrupted. I wasn't sure how to take her response to what he had said. She seemed mortified. *Maybe I should never tell her.*

Chapter 4

Caitlyn

I closed the door behind me and leaned against the mahogany wood. My head hit the door as my eyes closed, air catching in the middle of my throat. I had spent so much time with Wyatt over the years, but the time we spent together at the festival seemed different somehow. Had things shifted between us? *What was he goin' to say before Dyl opened the door?* I made a mental note to ask him the next time I saw him.

I pushed off the door and climbed the stairs to my bedroom. I loved everything about my room. Especially the IKEA furniture I'd built myself. Putting each piece together was one of my absolute favorite things. The only thing that would have made it better was to have Wyatt construct them with me. A small smile appeared on my lips as I let myself fall backward onto my bed with thoughts of Wyatt floating through my mind.

Dyl hadn't been too far off with his question about when Wyatt and I would start dating. I would have loved to have Wyatt as my boyfriend, but I wasn't going to saddle him with my disease. He deserved better. He deserved someone normal. And I didn't want to lose my best friend in the process. I was in trouble either way. Seeing him with someone else or losing him forever would shatter my heart.

"Don't you think that should be Wyatt's decision?" Mom's

voice echoed in my head.

We'd had that conversation last year when Mom had asked me why I didn't just tell him how I felt about him. Mom knew my feelings, I guess. Up to that point, I had never expressed them. Not out loud. To anyone. Until that day.

One day, I might get the courage to tell Wyatt how I really feel about him. Maybe. If I could move past the feeling of burdening him.

*　*　*

The next morning, I woke up ready to face the world head-on. It was Sunday. It was the Lord's day, and I couldn't wait to spend it with Him and the people He had brought into my life.

When I was dressed and ready to go, I took one last look in the mirror. I ran my fingers through my long hair before smoothing out my black, belted, knee-length dress. As I slipped my feet into my faux snakeskin ankle boots, I grabbed my keys, Bible, and purse off the dresser and bounded down the stairs.

On my way to church, I prayed that Emelia would finally be there. Even when I was away at school, I had prayed every Sunday since Quinn's death. Even though I hadn't been there to see it.

"All in Your timin', God. All in Your timin'," I uttered before pulling into a parking space in the lot outside of Lighthouse Community Church.

Pastor Steve stood outside, greeting everyone who entered, just as he had done every Sunday since he arrived as lead pastor at the church a few years before. "Good mornin', Caitlyn," he greeted me with an outstretched hand. "So nice to see you're home. Will you be stayin' long?"

"I'm back home, Pastor Steve. I've decided to become a

paramedic. Well, an EMT first." I grimaced as I wasn't sure how he would take the news.

"Well, we can always use more people like you servin' our community." He smiled before turning to the person standing behind me.

I stepped into the sanctuary and searched for Wyatt. When I spotted him in our usual row—on the right side of the church but smack dab in the middle of the section—I made my way up the aisle. The sunlight from the rising sun shone through the stained-glass window, causing a kaleidoscope of colors on the gray carpeted floor. I glanced up at the scene on the window portraying Jesus among children with his arms outstretched to them. I liked to think that was how Jesus looked when He welcomed Quinn home. I held back a tear that threatened the corner of my eye.

"Hey, Mom. Hey, Dad." I waved as I passed their pew.

My eyes moved to the people sitting in the pew behind Wyatt. I saw the dark-brown, shoulder-length hair and smiled. Emelia had come with Luke. My heart almost jumped out of my chest as my breath stopped for the slightest moment. I glanced at the ceiling as I silently gave thanks to God.

I stopped in the aisle and tried to maintain my composure as the excitement of seeing Emelia threatened to take over. "Hey, Emelia."

"Hey, Caitlyn. How are you?" She reached her arms out, and we embraced in a hug.

I hesitated to answer her question. While it seemed like a mundane and easy question to answer, I also knew that Emelia was still grieving the loss of her daughter. I was still grieving, too. "I'm hanging in there. How are you?"

"Doing the same." Emelia released me as she tried her best to smile. It barely registered on her face.

I patted her arm and took my place next to Wyatt in front of them. We always sat together at church. Shocker, I know. "Heya, Cowboy," I whispered as I leaned the side of my body into his, causing heat to sear through the sleeve of my sweater.

He leaned his head down and whispered, "Hey, Chipmunk. How are ya?"

"I'm good. Better now." I grinned up at him. *Stop flirting with him, Caitlyn.*

Pastor Steve took his place at the pulpit and began the service. He said a quick prayer and welcomed the worship team up to join him. Worship was my favorite part. I didn't have the greatest singing voice, but it wasn't completely horrible, either. Besides, God said to make a joyful noise, rejoice, and sing praise. So, that is what I always did.

I found that when I was feeling completely broken and didn't know what to say, I could sing a worship song, and the love of God would envelop me and fill my soul. There wasn't another feeling like it. Not even Wyatt's hugs. And he gave the BEST hugs ever.

When I heard the first few chords of *How Can It Be* by Lauren Daigle, my eyes instantly welled up with tears. I had heard Missy, the worship leader, sing it before, and she sang it beautifully.

I lifted my face and arms to heaven, closed my eyes, and allowed the song to wash over me. It was a song about doing things that don't glorify God and not understanding how God can still love us. God frees us from those things, and it's beyond our own understanding. How could God still love us in the times when we sin? How could He not turn His back on us when we disobey His commands?

Feelings of guilt started to bubble up for the anger I directed at God for taking so many people from me much too early in life—my grandpa, my two uncles, and Quinn. I wasn't sure my heart could take much more, yet in the midst of that song, I felt the presence of God wrap a warmth around me like a hug, and I'd never felt more loved. A tear fell to my cheek, and I thanked God for His infinite mercy, grace, and limitless love.

"You okay?" Wyatt whispered close to my ear as the song ended.

"Better than okay." I smiled and dried my cheeks with my fingertips.

The music ended, and we were all seated as Pastor Steve began speaking. The sermon was about forgiveness. My thoughts went to Emelia. I knew something had changed within her when I told her after the funeral that Quinn had accepted Jesus as her Savior, but I also knew she had so much to overcome. My hope and prayers were that she would finally get to a place where forgiveness would flow through her like a river. For Gary. For herself.

I also hoped and prayed she'd find happiness and joy again. With Luke. No one knew if she'd stay or if she'd leave. Everyone was just doing their best to give her grace and space to choose. We all wanted her to stay, but the decision was hers and hers alone.

Wyatt and I needed to decide what we wanted to do for Emelia to honor Quinn this Christmas. My first thought was to make lanterns out of sticks and biodegradable materials, put messages to Quinn on them, and send them out into the bay and to ask Mayor Travers if we could possibly plant a tree near the playground behind the lighthouse.

"Ya ready to go?" Wyatt asked me as he stood from the pew, breaking me free from my thoughts.

"It's over?" I shook my head to bring my mind fully back

to the present.

Wyatt chuckled. "Were you lost in your thoughts again?"

Heat burned my cheeks. "Yes, but I didn't think it'd been that long."

"Well, everyone is headed over to the café."

"What? Why?" My face scrunched in confusion as we rarely went to the café after church service.

Wyatt's face turned beet red. He was keeping something from me.

"Spill it, Cowboy." I stood with my hand on my hip.

"I can't." He bit his bottom lip before releasing it from his teeth and sticking it out in a pout. "Don't make me. I promised."

"Fine." I rolled my eyes. Wyatt had never broken a promise he'd made. He would never. "Let's go then." I grabbed his arm and pulled him outside. "Do ya wanna ride with me?" I asked.

He scanned our surroundings, sliding his hands down his thighs. "Um. I have to get back to the ranch to take care of some chores after."

My heart plummeted. "Oh. Okay."

As I drove the short distance to the café, my mind wandered once again. Had Mom and Dad planned something? I twirled a strand of hair around my index finger. They knew I hated being the center of attention, but when had that ever stopped them? My car rolled to a stop in front of the café. I inhaled and held it, expanding my lungs, and then blew out the breath with great exaggeration as I pulled the key from the ignition. "Here goes nothin'."

The party appeared to be in full swing with what seemed like everyone in town. I had never seen this many people in the café at one time. A huge *Welcome Home* sign hung on the wall above *Be Strong and Courageous.* Relief washed over me when no one yelled surprise as I plodded through the door.

"Caitlyn, it's so good to have you home." Marie and Carl approached me. Marie had her arms extended out to me, which I fell into once she was close enough.

"Thank you. It's good to be home." My eyes danced around the room at everyone who had gathered to welcome me home. I was truly blessed. *Why did I ever want to leave this place?* I found myself asking that over and over again.

It didn't take long for my eyes to find Wyatt. It never mattered how crowded a room was, my eyes would always find him. He was having a conversation with someone, but the person was hidden in the crowd. When a feminine hand reached out and touched his forearm, a tightness I'd never felt before grabbed hold of my chest, and a lump lodged itself in the center of my throat, strangling my breath. Tears stung my eyes.

I need air! I dashed for the door. The jingle bells knocked on the glass so hard that I thought I might have broken the pane. But their sound couldn't be heard over the music and conversation—or the sound of my heart beating out of my chest.

I sank down onto the cast-iron bench. The cool air hit my face like cold water, and I gasped for air as if I'd just been drowning. *What's wrong with you, Caitlyn? He can talk to other women. It's not like you've told him how you feel about him. This is the way* you *wanted it, remember?*

I knew I needed to tell Wyatt how I felt, but he deserved to be with someone like that woman he was talking to inside. Not someone like me, with a disease that could sometimes be unpredictable.

"Chipmunk, what are ya doin' out here?" Wyatt asked as he wrapped his jacket around my shoulders and pulled me from my internal confrontation.

I gulped. "Just needed some air."

"Sorry I didn't come over when ya came in. Delilah cornered me." Irritation dripped from his voice.

I waved my hand. "No worries."

"Do ya wanna just sit out here for a bit?"

Neither of us was a big fan of crowds. I smiled over at him. "I'd like that."

Wyatt grazed my shoulder with his fingertips as he draped his arm over the back of the bench. Goosebumps prickled my skin. I lay my head on his shoulder and basked in the comfortable silence.

Does he feel the same way about me? There's only one way to find out, Caitlyn. Maybe one day I'll find out. Why not now? "Cowboy, I—"

"What are you two doing out here?" Mom broke off my sentence as she rubbed the chill from her arms.

"Nothin'," I replied. "Just sittin' here. Why?"

"Everyone is ready for cake."

"Ooh." I licked my lips. No one made cake quite like Mom. At least, none I'd ever tasted.

Wyatt and I stood and followed Mom back to the party. Once inside, I shook Wyatt's jacket from my shoulders and handed it to him.

Dad wheeled the cake from the back. *Welcome Home* was scrawled across the top in light-pink icing against a white icing background. A Precious Moments figurine of two girls dancing was frozen in time just below the words. One blonde girl was bigger than the other blonde girl. Both were wearing similar pink and white dresses. Tears pricked my eyes as I knew they symbolized Quinn and me.

"Mom. Dad. It's beautiful." I swiped at my tears.

A gasp came from behind me. When I turned, Emelia was staring at the cake with her hand over her heart. Tears formed at each corner of her eyes. She squeezed my forearm. She saw the resemblance also.

"It really is beautiful." Emelia enveloped me in a hug. "I'm so glad you're home."

"Me, too."

"Save some hugs for me," Uncle Colt called out.

"And me," Aunt Callie followed.

"Can we cut the cake already?" Dyl chimed in.

The café filled with laughter. Yes. It was good to be back home, surrounded by so many amazing people. I gazed up at Wyatt as he stood beside me.

Well, I almost told him. When the time is right, I'll try again.

Mom slipped a piece of paper into my hand just before I excused myself to the bathroom. When the door was locked, I unfolded the paper. I smiled. Mom had written down all of the information I needed to determine how much insulin I needed to take. I knew I would have to stare at the delicious goodness for fifteen minutes, but it was worth the wait.

I returned to the party and sat at a table next to Wyatt, which caused Delilah's daggers to burn right through me. She had always had a crush on him. Since the day he started at our school. It did make me wonder why he never went out with her.

"I got you a piece of cake." Wyatt pushed a plate toward me.

"Thank you." I smiled as I caught a glimpse of the corner piece in front of me. He knew me too well. The corner piece had always been my favorite. The perfect icing-to-cake ratio.

Wyatt leaned in close. So close I could feel his breath on

my ear. Chills spread throughout my body. "So, have you thought more about the gift for Emelia?" he asked.

"I have so many ideas. I was thinkin' of lanterns on the bay, but I want to do somethin' that is safer for the environment and the animals, so maybe pinwheels? Pink and white ones. I was also thinkin' of askin' Mayor Travers if we could plant a tree in town."

"Those sound like great ideas. I love how your face lights up when you talk about it."

Heat rushed to my cheeks. I noticed eyes were on us. "We can talk more about it later. When there aren't any ears to hear."

Wyatt smiled. "Sounds good." He plopped a bite of cake in his mouth before pointing his fork at his plate. "This really is the best cake."

I glanced over at Mom and Dad. "It really is." I picked up my fork and slid it through the partial pink flower on my slice, the strawberry flavor tickling my tongue as the icing melted in my mouth.

People soon began filing out the door, but not before stopping to say goodbye to me as I was clearing off the tables.

"I got this, Mom and Dad. Why don't you both go home and relax?" I took the plates from their hands.

"We can't leave you to clean all this up after your own party," Mom argued.

Wyatt chimed in, "I can help."

"Are you sure?" Dad asked me.

"Of course. Thank you so much for the party. I had a really good time." I hugged each of them with my free arm.

Mom sighed. "Okay then. See you at home."

Dad wrapped his arm around Mom's shoulders as they walked out the door.

Wyatt started picking up plates off the tables. "This place isn't gonna clean itself."

I placed my hand on his arm. "Thank you for helpin' me. You don't have to stay, though. If you don't want to."

"Tryin' ta get rid of me, are ya?" He held his hand to his heart.

"I just didn't know if you had other plans . . . with Delilah." I cringed at the taste of her name on my tongue. "Or if you needed to get back to your chores."

Wyatt grinned, and his cheeks pinkened. "I only said that because I wanted the surprise to be all about you. And as far as Delilah goes, I don't want to hang out with her. I'm all yours." He cleared his throat. "For the rest of the evenin'."

My heart thudded at his *I'm all yours* comment. "Well, we'd better get to it then." I stacked some plates in the dish bin Mom had placed on one of the tables before she left.

After we gathered all the dishes, Wyatt carried the bin into the kitchen and set it in the sink. Then, he turned in my direction. "I'll dry if you wash."

"Okay." I smiled.

Most places had heavy-duty dishwashing equipment, but not the café. Mom and Dad thought it was more important to have better ovens, refrigerators, and stoves. Those had needed replacing all within close proximity to each other, but Mom and Dad were saving up to buy proper equipment. I couldn't disagree, but doing the dishes was one of my least favorite things. At least having Wyatt there made it more bearable. He was the first to slice through the silence. "So, tell me more about these pinwheels for Quinn."

Excitement surged through me. "Well, I was thinking we could plant a tree near the playground across from the bay, and we could make pinwheels and write notes to Quinn on them.

We could place them around the tree. Like I said, they'd be pink and white. Quinn's favorite colors." I took in a breath and exhaled. "So, what do ya think?"

"I think that sounds like a great idea. I think Quinn would love it, too. So, I think Emelia will also."

A satisfied grin spread across my face as I sank my hands in the hot, soapy water. Internally, I did a little happy dance. "Now, I just have to talk to Mayor Travers and ask if I can do it."

"I could go with you." Wyatt quickly clamped his mouth shut but then opened it to say, "Ya, know. If ya want. But no big deal if ya don't." His shoulder lifted to his cheek, which was tinged the slightest shade of pink.

"I'd like that," I admitted a little too freely for my liking. "I'll call tomorrow to see when I can get an appointment."

"Just let me know." Wyatt lifted the plate from my hands and began drying it.

When the last dish was washed, dried, and put away, disappointment flooded my body. I sighed. "I guess that's it."

"Yeah." Wyatt exhaled deeply.

Is he just as disappointed as I am?

There really wasn't any way to prolong our time together. We were done cleaning up, and both of our cars were outside the café. As I opened the door, the jingle bells signaled the finality of our night. The tune did not reflect the sadness I felt as I slid the key into the lock and turned it.

I turned to Wyatt. "Be safe drivin' home."

Wrapping his arms around me, he said, "I will. You, too."

I wrapped my arms around his middle. "Text when ya get home?"

"Always do." His arms dropped from my shoulders, and a chill enveloped me. "Let me know when you're goin' to see

Mayor Travers."

"I will."

"Night, Chipmunk."

"Night, Cowboy."

I could feel his eyes on me as I stepped off the curb to get to my car. It was just like him to wait until I was safely on my way home before leaving himself. Such a gentleman. A dreamy sigh escaped my lips.

I checked my rearview mirror, and sure enough, he was standing on the sidewalk with his hands in his pockets, watching me drive away. My heart fluttered.

* * *

The next day, I could hardly contain my excitement. I dialed the number to the mayor's office before I even got out of bed and ready for the day.

"Good morning, Mayor Travers's office. Mary speaking. How may I assist you today?"

"Hi, Mary. This is Caitlyn Logan. I was hoping I could schedule an appointment to talk to Mayor Travers." I bit the tip of my nail on my index finger.

"What would this be regarding?"

"I wanted to ask if I could plant a tree in town in honor of Quinn Taylor."

"Well, I can tell you, you'd have to get it approved by the town council."

"The problem is, I don't want the person it's for to find out." Disappointment began to swirl.

"Meeting agendas are full until after Christmas."

I sighed deeply. "Okay. Thank you." I hit End and threw my phone on my bed as tears stung my eyes. *What am I gonna do now?* I closed my eyes and emptied my lungs of all the air they held. As I opened my eyes and drew in another breath, I picked the phone back up and hit Wyatt's name with my thumb.

"Hey, Chipmunk. What's up?"

"Hey, Cowboy," I greeted him solemnly.

"Uh oh. What's wrong?"

"The mayor's office said I'd have to get permission for the tree from the town council at the monthly meeting, and there isn't an opening in the agenda until after Christmas." I groaned. "I don't know what to do now."

"Aww. I'm sorry." He paused. I could hear his teeth grinding. He always did that when he was thinking. "Hey. Why don't you ask Colt if we can plant it at the ranch? It was Quinn's favorite place, after all."

"Oh. That's a great idea!" My excitement slowly returned. "I'll see you in a little bit."

"Awesome. See ya soon."

I hit End and jumped from my bed, hurrying to get dressed. I chose a pink sweatshirt and a pair of jeans. Wyatt always said pink was his favorite color on me. Of course, I pulled on my worn brown cowgirl boots. I quickly pulled my hair into a high ponytail and took my morning dose of insulin.

When I arrived at the ranch, my palms started to sweat. *What if Uncle Colt says no?* I shook my head. *It's for Quinn and Emelia. He won't say no.* I breathed in and out heavily before getting out of my car.

Callie's voice carried from the stable.

"Hey, Aunt Callie," I said as I stepped inside.

"Oh, hey, Caitlyn. What brings you by?" She didn't turn away from or stop massaging Warrior.

"I was hoping to talk to Uncle Colt about somethin'." I twisted a strand of hair between my fingers.

"He's out on Beauty. You can tack up Minnie if you want."

"Really?"

"Sure. I'll help." Aunt Callie grabbed the saddle from the sawhorse. "So, what do you want to talk to Colt about?"

Heat rushed to my cheeks as we buckled the saddle around Minnie. "I'd like to keep that a secret for now. At least until Uncle Colt tells me yes or no."

Disappointment filled Aunt Callie's eyes and could be heard in her voice. "Sure. No problem."

I climbed up into the saddle and motioned Minnie to walk out of the stable. *Wonder where Uncle Colt could be.* "I guess we could check the fence line first, Minnie." I patted her neck.

I tugged gently on the reins to get Minnie moving in the right direction and tapped my feet against her sides to get her going. As we crested the first hill, I saw Uncle Colt and Beauty trotting in our direction. I raised my hand high over my head and waved.

"Hey, Caitlyn. What are ya doin' here? Hey there, Minnie," Uncle Colt greeted us as they approached.

"Well, I needed to ask ya somethin', and I'm runnin' outta time."

"What's up?" He rested his arm on the horn of his saddle as Beauty lowered her head to graze on some grass. Minnie followed Beauty's lead.

"Well, I want to do somethin' for Emelia for Christmas, to honor Quinn."

"Oh? That'll be nice. I'm sure she'd like and appreciate that. What'd ya have in mind?"

I bit my fingernail. "So, I wanted to plant a tree and make pink and white pinwheels to put around the tree. Originally, I wanted to do it in town, but I can't seek approval from the town council until after Christmas. So, I was hopin' you'd let me do it here?"

Uncle Colt tilted his head and looked up at the sky as if in contemplation. "Well . . . I think we can make that happen."

"Really?" Hope rose into my heart.

"Of course. Why don't ya pick a spot for the tree and let me know where. Can we let Callie and Luke in on the surprise? We might need more hands."

"Ya don't think they'd let it slip to her, do ya?"

"Not if we tell 'em it's a surprise. They kept your party a secret from ya, didn't they? Twice even." Uncle Colt grinned.

"Good point. I don't see why not, then. I'll see if Wyatt wants to help me find the perfect spot." My smile spread across my face.

"Sounds like a good plan." Uncle Colt glanced over his shoulder. "I guess I'd better get back to the fence. Looks like there are a couple of places that need some work. Keep me updated."

"I will. Thank you, Uncle Colt."

"No problem." He pulled on the reins, and Beauty turned back toward the fence before trotting off.

Giddiness overtook me as I motioned Minnie toward the stable. On the ride back, I closed my eyes and breathed in the fresh air as the crispness of the wind kissed my face. It didn't take long before the stable came into view, as we hadn't ventured very far.

"Back so soon?" Aunt Callie called out from the doorway of the stable.

I smiled down at her. "Yeah. Didn't have to go too far to find them."

"So, do I ever get to hear the secret?" she asked as I jumped down from the saddle.

"Well, can you keep a secret from Emelia?"

"Um. I kept secrets from you, didn't I?" She raised a brow. If it wasn't for the smile on Aunt Callie's face, I would have thought she was offended.

"I suppose that's true." I led Minnie into the stable and grabbed a brush from the wall and explained my plan to Aunt Callie. I exhaled deeply. "So, what do ya think? Is it too much? Too soon? Do ya think Emelia would like it?"

With tears in her eyes, Aunt Callie said, "I think she will love it. It'll be hard for her, but it's a really beautiful idea that she'll appreciate." She touched my forearm with her fingertips. "I'd better get back to the house. You staying for lunch?"

"No. I want to do some research on EMT classes. Don't want to put it off too long."

"Okay. Hope you'll join us again soon."

"I will. I promise. Do ya know where Wyatt is? Wanted to say hi before I left."

"I think he's running errands with Luke."

Disappointment raided my insides. "Oh. Okay. I'll finish up with Minnie and head home then."

"Okay. See you next time."

"Bye, Aunt Callie."

I finished brushing Minnie in silence and solitude before returning her to her stall. I sighed heavily because I hadn't seen Wyatt. I always looked forward to seeing him whenever I came to the ranch.

I wonder if Uncle Colt will let me move here. What? Where'd that come from? Not a bad idea, though. *I'll have to pray about it and talk to Mom and Dad. And Uncle Colt, of course.*

Chapter 5

Wyatt

"**C**aitlyn stopped by today," Callie informed me as she passed the bowl of roasted potatoes.

"Oh?" I raised a brow. I ignored the slight rise in my heart rate at the mention of her name.

"She was pretty sad when she didn't get to see you." Callie grinned.

What's she grinnin' like that for? My eyebrows furrowed. "Well, I'm sad I missed her, too."

I wanted to ask Colt if Caitlyn had talked to him and what he'd told her, but not with Emelia sitting across from me, her face partially blocked by the vase of fresh flowers on the table, no doubt placed there by Callie. I had to keep my mouth shut. Caitlyn would never forgive me if I let that secret out.

I ate my food in silence as conversations all around me pricked my ears. I hadn't lied when I said I had missed her, too. My time with Caitlyn was always the best and most fulfilling. *Maybe I'll ask Colt about Chipmunk's request after dinner.*

At the café the night before, as we were sitting on the bench, just being, I almost got up the nerve to tell Caitlyn how I felt. It felt so good and natural with my arm on the back of the bench—kind of around her. Especially when she rested her head on my shoulder. When we can do that every night until the end of time, it will be a wonderful time. *One day it will happen.* Just needed to face my fears and blurt it out. One day. I sighed.

"You've been awfully quiet tonight," Colt said, intruding upon my thoughts.

When my eyes focused on the room around me, everyone had already gotten up from the table.

"Last one up has to help me with the dishes." Colt chuckled.

I smirked. "Seems I've had to do my fair share of dishes lately. Well, last night really doesn't count, I guess, because I did them with Caitlyn."

"Oh. Still sweet on my niece, huh?"

How does he know that? I've never told anyone about my feelings for her.

As if reading my mind, Colt said, "It's written all over your face. Still haven't told her?" He let some dishes slip under the soapy water as I grabbed a towel.

I sighed. "No." Then, I opened my mouth, and all the words fell out. "She deserves so much better than me. She's gorgeous and sweet. And I'm . . . me. And she's my best friend. Not sure I could handle rejection from her and lose my best friend all at the same time."

Colt stopped washing a dish and turned toward me. I watched as the plate disappeared beneath the suds. "Wyatt, how can you even say she deserves better than you? I can't imagine someone better for her *than* you. You're strong, compassionate, kind, loving . . . do I need to go on?"

Heat radiated my cheeks. Those words had never been spoken to or about me before. "No."

"Not to mention, I've seen how she looks at you. There's no way she'd reject ya."

I scratched the back of my head. "Ya really think so?"

"I do." Colt handed me the last dish.

I glanced behind me to make sure no one else was there. "So, did she talk to you today?"

He nodded. "She did."

"And?" I shifted my weight from foot to foot. The suspense was killing me.

"I gave her my blessin'. She just needs to tell me where and when and if she needs my help with anythin'."

"Awesome." A smile spread across my lips.

"Thanks for helpin' with the dishes." Colt took the towel from my hands and hung it on the oven door handle. He patted my shoulder. "Ready to go finish chores?"

"Yep." *No.*

All I really wanted to do was call Caitlyn and talk to her about the surprise. But *"responsibilities come first,"* Colt's voice floated through my head. The horses counted on us. I followed Colt to the corral to get the horses in the stable for the night.

"Hey, Flash. Ready to go in for the night?" I asked. He moved his head away when I tried to connect the lead. "Come on, buddy." I tried again, and Flash ran to the other side of the corral.

"What's wrong with him?" Colt asked as he walked over with Minnie.

Flash whinnied and reared up on his hind legs. When his front legs stomped back on the ground, he motioned with his nose toward the woods on the backside of the corral. A faint cry drifted through the air.

"Did ya hear that?" My eyes darted to Colt.

Colt unhooked the lead from Minnie. "Yeah. Let's go have a look."

We jogged into the woods. The moon was starting to rise

in the sky, casting shadows from the trees. Up above, an owl hooted through the darkness. A whinny sounded from our left.

"Over here, Colt." I moved closer to the area where I'd heard the sound. "It's getting louder in this direction, so we must be close."

When the trees cleared, we found a light-brown horse with a dark-brown mane and tail. He was beautiful. The moon was at just the right angle in a small opening in the treetops, creating a stream of light that landed right on the animal. It was something out of a fantasy movie.

Colt kneeled at the base of a tree and motioned for me to do the same. "Well, I'll be." He scratched his head. "How did he get all the way over here?"

"What do you mean?"

"This might be a Corolla Mustang. If it is, he's really far from home."

The Corolla Mustangs lived in the Outer Banks, some ninety-six miles away.

"What makes you think he is one of them?"

"Well, do you see how he's shorter than our horses?"

"Yeah."

"And how his tail is lower?"

A coyote howled in the distance as a twig snapped under my foot. I inhaled and held my breath. The horse's nostrils flared, and the whites of his eyes glowed. He hobbled in a circle but did not attempt to flee. He curled his left hoof under him.

"His foot or leg may be broken," Colt whispered.

I pointed toward the horse's hind end. "I see, but look at that."

"What is it?" Colt gasped. "Holy . . ."

The horse turned, and his hindquarters glistened in the moonlight.

"I'm gonna see if I can get a closer look." Colt stood from his crouched position. "You stay here until I can see if I can get the horse under my control."

I held my breath as Colt approached the horse. The horse looked spooked but didn't attempt to run. If I'd had to guess, I'd say it was because of his foot or those lacerations on his hind, or maybe both. Colt held his hands up in the air so that the horse knew he meant no harm.

"It's okay, boy. I'm not here to hurt you. I just want to help." Colt looked him over. Then, he turned his face toward me. "I can't tell for sure, but it looks like maybe he was mauled. I can't see it clearly enough to know for sure."

"How are we gonna get him out of here? He'll be bait out here alone."

A howl came from the right of us . . . a lot closer than it had been. My heart rate quickened. He would definitely be bait to that coyote.

"I'm gonna try and put the lead around his neck." Colt put the loop up to the horse's nose, and the horse sniffed it. "See? It's okay. It's not gonna hurt ya." Colt placed the rope under the horse's nose and attempted to loop the other part of the rope so that it would be on top of his nose. The horse reared up as much as he could before he stomped down. Colt fell out of the way just before the horse's hoof hit the ground. "Woah, that was close," Colt huffed. He stood and dusted off his pants before sliding the rope back in place. This time, the horse didn't move. "That's it. It's not gonna hurt ya. Neither am I."

Colt let the rope sit on the horse's nose before moving it a little higher. "Good boy." He lifted the rope over the horse's ears and let it fall to his neck before tightening it enough that it wouldn't come off. "Come on, boy. We need to get you to a safe place so we can have a look at ya. I know it's gonna be painful, but I can't leave ya out here all alone. Not with that coyote comin'."

Colt gently pulled on the rope. His mouth formed an "o" when the horse moved to follow him, limping as we went.

I expelled the air I'd been holding in. "Wow. That was a lot easier than I thought it would be."

"Except for the part where he almost trampled me." Colt blew out a breath. "But yeah. I think he's been out here for a while. He looks like he was almost ready to give up. We need to get Doc Norris out here."

As we made our way into the clearing beside the corral, I pulled my phone from my pocket, scrolled to Doc's number, and tapped it.

"You have reached the voicemail of Dr. Norris, Edenton Animal Hospital Veterinarian. I'm unable to take your call at this time. If this is an emergency, please press 1." I tapped the number and lifted the phone back to my ear. "Please leave your name, phone number, and the nature of your emergency, and the doctor will be paged to return your call. Thank you."

Beep.

I steadied my voice. "Doc, this is Wyatt Glover at Redemption Ranch. We found what may be a wild horse in the woods with some serious injuries. Please call me back, or call Colt. Thanks." I sighed and hit End before dropping my phone in my back pocket.

"Hopefully, he'll call back soon." Worry dripped from Colt's voice.

When we arrived at the stable and stepped into the light, I noticed the horse had large claw marks on his hind end. "What do ya make of that?" My heart ached for him.

"Not sure."

My phone vibrated in my pocket. I'd turned the ringer off

and had forgotten to turn it back on. I heaved a sigh of relief. The last thing we needed was for the phone to scare the already terrified animal.

"This is Wyatt," I spoke into the phone as I held it up to my ear.

"Wyatt, this is Dr. Norris. I'm on my way."

"Great." Relief washed over me for what seemed like the millionth time that night. "We were able to get the horse to the stable."

"Really?" Surprise filled the vet's voice. "I'll be there as quickly as I can."

"Thanks, Doc." I turned to Colt as I shoved my phone back into my pocket. "Doc is on his way."

"Good. We just have to keep the horse calm until he gets here."

"I'm gonna go check on Flash and Minnie," I said.

"Good idea. They should be fine in the corral until we get this one settled."

When I stepped out of the stable, Flash and Minnie were at the fence with their noses over the top beam. I could feel their worry as I got closer to them.

"It's okay." I rubbed the side of Flash's head. "Good boy for letting us know about him. Hopefully, we got to him in time."

I patted both horses on the side before heading back to the stable. A vehicle door slammed just as my foot landed inside.

"Doc's here," Colt said.

"I heard. Oh, hey, Doc." I greeted the vet with the white handlebar mustache and matching white hair. He reminded me of the doctor in *Field of Dreams*. That movie was ingrained in my head as it was one of Jon's favorites. We had watched it too many times to count.

"So, what do we have here?"

"Looks like he was mauled by somethin' but not entirely sure what," I said.

Doc Norris set his medical bag on the floor and slowly leaned in to take a closer look at the horse's wounds. He lowered his glasses on his nose and studied the injuries. "Looks like it could have possibly been a black bear. We've had some sightings, and if the bear was hungry enough . . ." Doc sighed. "I've got some antibiotics in the truck and the ingredients to make some salve. Let me rustle some up right quick."

"How old do ya think he is?" Colt asked.

"Well, let's see if he'll let me have a look." Doc stood off to the side of the horse so the animal could keep Doc in his sight. Doc slowly lifted his hands to the horse's mouth and gently moved his lips to reveal his teeth. "He has his canine teeth, as you can see right here. So, that makes him about four or five years old."

"Oh, wow. So young to be so far away from home and all alone. Makes you really wonder what happened to him." Colt rubbed the back of his neck.

"Okay. Let me go get what I need from my truck. I'll be right back." Doc patted the horse before turning and walking out the door.

"A black bear. Wow," I said in awe when Doc was out of sight.

"Yeah. I heard some rumblin's about a black bear when I was at the feed store last week. Never heard of an attack, though. Course, never heard of a wild horse 'round here, either." Colt shrugged.

"Crazy night for sure." I lifted my hat from my head, ran my hand through my hair, and plopped it back on my head.

"Okay." Doc shuffled back in. "Here's the salve. Ya need

to clean the wounds two times a day with copious amounts of water and soap. Put the salve on in a generous amount, then cover them with these bandages. It doesn't look like the puncture wounds were deep enough to warrant stitches, but I'll come by and check on him tomorrow."

Doc stepped from the horse's view, removed a syringe from his pocket, and uncapped it. He stuck the needle into the horse's rear end and injected the medicine. The horse didn't move an inch. He really was on the edge of giving up. Poor guy. "He's so docile for a wild horse, and he appears a little malnourished," Dr. Norris noted.

Colt stepped toward the horse. "He looked like he was close to giving up when we found him. Oh, he was also favorin' his left front leg."

"Well, let's have a look." Doc shifted to the front of the horse. He moved his hands up and down, gently massaging. "Looks like a sprain. Doesn't feel like anythin' is broken. I have some support bandagin' in the truck. You'll want to use hot and cold compresses as well."

"Okay. We have those, I believe." Colt lifted his eyes to the ceiling as if in contemplation.

"If you don't, let me know. I'll bring some out tomorrow. Let me go get those bandages right quick."

Colt and I waited in silence.

When Doc returned to the stable, he said, "Okay. Here ya go. Call me if anythin' changes. Especially if he gets worse. I'll give ya a call tomorrow."

"Thanks, Doc. Really appreciate ya comin' out," I said.

"Of course. Of course. Have a good night, guys." Doc waved before disappearing into the darkness.

"Well, I guess I'd better get started," Colt said. "You can go ahead and go, Wyatt. You've helped enough. I'm sure you're exhausted."

"I'd like to stay and help. If that's okay."

"Sure. That'd be great. Thanks."

After applying the salve and wrapping the wounds, along with wrapping the front leg, Colt suggested, "We should put him in the paddock. I think the fence will be high enough. Even though he has a bum leg, I don't want to take any chances. We'll start with the hot and cold compresses tomorrow. I just have to remember where I put them."

We walked the horse the short distance to the paddock, and Colt closed the gate behind him. The horse began limping around the fence of the paddock in a circle. Colt scratched his head. "We're gonna need everyone's help, so I'll address that at breakfast in the mornin'. For now, let's get Minnie and Flash back in the stable and get some shut-eye."

Once Minnie and Flash were back in their stalls, Colt and I parted ways for the night. As I began walking to my cabin, I turned back to the paddock. The new horse was pacing back and forth. He looked so lost and confused. And lonely. I knew all those feelings well . . . too well. I reversed my direction and went back to him.

"Hey, buddy." I stepped up to the fence surrounding him, my arms resting on the beam. "You look a little sad and confused. Miss your momma, huh?"

The horse's eyes focused on me. He didn't move away or come any closer. He just stood in the center of the ring. Frozen.

"Why are you out here all alone and so far from home? I know what that feels like. My mom and dad used to leave me for days at a time. For a long time, I didn't know why. I eventually found out it was because of drugs. When I was thirteen, they left me for good. I didn't know where to go, how to get food, or if I'd ever feel safe. I wasn't even sure I knew what it meant to feel safe."

The horse slowly started toward me but stopped when I stopped talking to him.

"Is that what happened to you? Did you lose your mom and dad? Did you not know where to go or how to get food?"

Before I'd finished my last question, the horse nuzzled his nose against my hand hanging inside the fence. Chills spread throughout my body. My breath hitched in my throat. *A wild horse is touching me! Wait till I tell Chipmunk.* A wide smile that I thought would never fade spread across my face.

"Can I take a picture of you to send to Chipmunk? She's gonna love ya. She's the best person ever. You're gonna love her, too."

The horse lifted his head. I aimed my phone at him and snapped a picture. When the light flashed, fear filled his eyes. He reared up and let out a shrill cry.

"I'm so sorry. I didn't think about the flash. I'm so sorry."

"What's goin' on out here?" Colt shouted as he ran up to the fence.

"It's all my fault. I wanted to take a picture of him to send to Chip— Caitlyn. I didn't think about the flash goin' off and scarin' him." I lowered my head. "I feel awful."

"It's okay, Wyatt." Colt patted my shoulder. "Accidents happen. We all just have to be mindful that he's a wild horse, and he's in an unfamiliar place. And locked in a cage, so to speak."

"Yeah." My head and shoulders slumped. "So, are we gonna name him?"

"I don't know. My plan is to return him to the wild, but I'm not sure if that will be possible. Let's hold off for now. In a few days, I'm gonna call the Corolla Wild Horse Fund and see if he is one of theirs. If not, I'll see if they can take him once he's healed. They may even want to take him before then." Colt shrugged. "Not sure. But we'll cross that road when we come to it. Now, go get some sleep." Colt patted my shoulder once more.

"Okay. Night, Colt."

"Night, Wyatt."

I trudged to my cabin with heavy, slow steps. *You're so stupid, Wyatt. Next time, use your brain.* My dad's voice drifted through my mind. Weird. I hadn't heard his raspy, drug-induced slurred speech in years.

I shook my head as I turned the knob and entered my cabin. My eyes lifted to the clock on the wall: 11 p.m. No wonder I was so exhausted. I wanted to tell Caitlyn about the horse. But first . . . a shower.

Chapter 6

Caitlyn

Sitting on my bed, I was able to see my entire room. I loved the color pink. My room was mostly black and white but with a splash of pink mixed in from my light-pink pillow, my pink bear, and my soft ballerina doll with hot-pink tutu and shoes. I ran my hand along my white bedspread with white ruffles. It had some silver sparkly accents, too.

My phone vibrated, telling me I had a text message. I plucked the phone from its resting place as I sank into my black pillows. Wyatt's name appeared on the screen, and a smile came to my lips. I unlocked the phone and tapped his name.

> *Hey, Chipmunk. How are ya? I'm sorry I missed ya earlier. But guess what? Colt and I found a hurt wild horse. Can ya believe it?*

> *Wow! That's crazy. Is it okay? Can I come see it?*

> *I don't see why not. Why are ya still awake? It's after midnight.*

A photo appeared. It was of a gorgeous, chestnut-brown horse with a dark-brown tail and short dark mane. It looked young.

Just couldn't sleep. Lot on my mind. How old is the horse? It's beautiful.

Doc Norris said he looks to be about five years old.

Man, that's young to be all by himself.

Yeah, Doc gave us some salve and gave him an antibiotic shot. He has a sprain in his front leg. It's gonna be a lot of work to get him back to 100 percent.

I bet. I'd love to help.

I'm sure Colt would let ya. I'd best get some sleep, though. Just wanted to tell ya about him.

I'd better, too.

Sweet dreams, Chipmunk.

Sweet dreams, Cowboy.

I plugged my charger into my phone and set it on my side table. Grabbing my bear, I squeezed him close and snuggled into my bed.

* * *

The next morning, I woke up with excitement bubbling inside me. I was going to see a wild horse, but I was also going to see Wyatt. My heart fluttered. After I got dressed and took my insulin, I all but ran down the stairs.

"Hey, Sis. Where are you off to in such a hurry?"

"Oh, hey, Dad. I'm goin' to the ranch. They found a wild horse last night."

"Wild horse? Here?" Dad's eyebrows rose to the middle of his forehead before one of them furrowed into his eye.

"Yep. That's what Wyatt texted me."

"Wow. Might have to drive out to see it. But for now, have fun and be careful. Will you be home for supper?" Dad wiped his hands on a white towel before he flipped it onto his shoulder.

"I'm not sure. I'll call if I'm gonna be late or miss supper." I had my hand on the doorknob of the front door. "Love you!"

"Love you, too," I heard just before I closed the door behind me.

I jumped into my car, blasted a Christian radio station, and barreled over to the ranch. It was about an eighteen-minute drive out there. I did my best not to speed . . . *too* much. Seeing Wyatt always excited me, but seeing the horse made the excitement heightened.

As I drove up the dirt road—more a path, really—and pulled up to the stable, to my right, I spotted the most majestic horse I'd ever seen. He was smaller than Minnie, but he fascinated me at first sight. He moved slowly around the circular paddock. He looked as if he wanted to run but couldn't figure it out with his hurt leg.

When I parked in front of the stable, Wyatt was already standing in the doorway. Looking mighty handsome, I might add. I pressed my hand to my heart as it skipped a beat. It usually did, especially when he smiled that smile I loved so much. It was a crooked grin, where only one side of his mouth turned up.

"Hey," I said as I stood from my car.

"Hey, you."

I pointed my thumb over my shoulder. "Is that him?"

"It is. Do ya wanna meet him?"

"Of course I do." I smiled wide.

"Well, alright. Let's go."

I followed Wyatt over to the paddock. The horse stopped pacing. I could tell he was watching us . . . waiting. Waiting on what, I wasn't sure.

"Hey, boy." Wyatt held his hand out to him.

The horse turned his head toward us.

"Colt doesn't want to name him because the plan is to return him to the wild. But it feels weird not givin' him a name. I guess he doesn't want anyone to get too attached. I dunno." Wyatt shrugged.

"Aww. Everyone needs a name."

The horse slowly made his way over to us and laid his nose in Wyatt's outstretched hand.

"Oh, my gosh," I whispered. "That's amazin'. Do you think he'd let me pet him?"

"I'm not sure. You can try. Just hold out your hand like I did."

I jammed my hand through the fence faster and with more force than I meant. The horse jumped before limping in the opposite direction. I covered my mouth with my fingers as tears pricked my eyes. "I'm so sorry. I got too excited."

A sheepish grin washed over Wyatt's face. "It's okay. Just like Colt told me last night, accidents happen. When I took the picture I sent you, the flash scared him."

"Aww. Poor boy. Well, maybe one day he'll let me. I'll let him decide, but I'd love to help take care of him."

"Well, I think Colt's doin' some work in the house. Wanna go ask him?"

I bounced up and down with excitement. "Yes."

"Come on." Wyatt curled his arm toward his shoulder.

As we approached the house, Uncle Colt was up on an aluminum ladder, cleaning out the gutters. "Hey, Uncle Colt!" I hollered up to him.

He turned his head as he grabbed onto the ladder with both hands to steady himself. "Oh, hey, Caitlyn. I didn't know you were comin' by today." He started to descend the steps.

"I wanted to see the horse, but I also wanted to talk to ya about somethin'."

"Oh?" He wiped his hands on his pants. "Well, come on in. Let's have some tea and chat."

Uncle Colt set three glasses of sweet tea on the table and sat down in a chair on the opposite side. "So, what's up?" He took a swig from his glass.

"Well." I bit my bottom lip as I twirled a piece of my hair. "Two things, actually. One, I wanted to see if I could help take care of the horse. And two, I wanted to ask if there was any way I could move into one of the cabins here." I inhaled and held it in. My fingers tightened around the strand of hair.

"Hmm." Uncle Colt peered past us, as if pondering my request. "Well, I don't see why ya can't help with the horse. Have ya been lookin' into EMT classes?" His left eyebrow made its way to the middle of his forehead as his right one lowered.

Heat rose to my cheeks. *What does that have to do with me movin' to the ranch?* "Um. A little? I'm just tryin' to unwind and enjoy the holiday season. You know it's my favorite. My plan is to get started after the first of the year. I promise."

Uncle Colt always acted like my third parent. Sometimes, it grated on my nerves, but I loved him so much that it mostly didn't bother me. I knew he did it because he loved me just as much.

"Have ya asked your mom and dad?"

"No. I wanted to talk to you first. To make sure it was even possible before I asked them." I wound the strand of hair around my index finger.

"Well, if it's okay with them, I don't see a problem with it. Wyatt can help ya get a cabin ready." He coughed. "I mean, if he wants to."

I wiggled in my seat and giggled with happiness.

"But!" He held up his index finger. "After you ask them, and after they say yes."

I let out a screech and I bolted from my chair, knocking it to the floor. I scurried around the table and flung my arms around Uncle Colt. "Thank you. Thank you. Thank you."

He patted my arm and chuckled. "Don't thank me yet. Your parents still have to say yes. Now, go before I change my mind."

Wyatt picked up my chair and scooted both chairs into the table. I grabbed him by the hand and pulled him out of the house. I jumped down from the porch and twirled around in circles before throwing my arms around him and screeching, "I'm so excited!"

"I can tell." He laughed.

I pried myself from his arms. "Now, to get Mom and Dad to say yes."

"Ya never told me ya wanted to move here." His voice was filled with sadness. "Kinda like ya didn't tell me ya quit school and were comin' home."

I studied his face. Had I really not told him? "I'm sorry, Cowboy. I should have told ya." I wrapped my arms around his waist. When he didn't do the same, I let go. "I hadn't planned on askin' him today. But I've wanted to live on this ranch my whole life. The opportunity to ask just hadn't happened. Until now. Should we go pick my cabin?"

"Shouldn't ya ask first?" He stood with his hands on his waist.

"Maybe. But I still wanna pick one. Please?" I folded my hands under my chin and stuck out my bottom lip.

Wyatt held his hands up in surrender. "Okay. Okay. Not the pouty lip."

"Yay! Thank you." Before I knew what I was doing, my lips connected with his cheek. I jumped away as if I'd been burned with hot coffee.

We walked to the cabins in silence.

What were ya thinkin', Caitlyn? Obviously, you weren't. How could you not tell your best friend about school before everyone else? What a dumb thing to do.

"So, what one do ya want?" Wyatt asked as we stood staring at the individual cabins. "There are only two empty ones. This one and the one next to mine."

That was a no-brainer for me. Living next to him was the next best thing to actually sharing one with him. My cheeks warmed at the thought. "Would you mind havin' me as a neighbor?"

"Nah, I wouldn't mind."

My heart plummeted with disappointment as I thought he would give a more excitement-filled reaction. "Well, I guess I should go ask Mom and Dad," I said with less enthusiasm. My heart was like a deflating balloon swirling through the air.

"Okay. Want me to walk ya to your car?"

"No. I'm all right. I know the way, and I'm sure you have chores to finish up anyway."

"Okay. Let me know what your mom and dad say."

"I will. Talk to you later." I started down the path before there was any more awkwardness. Like that was even possible. I wrapped my arms around my middle.

Maybe movin' to the ranch is a bad idea, I thought as I drove myself home. *Cowboy didn't seem too excited about the idea, especially when I asked about the cabin next to his. Maybe I just need to stay on track and look at EMT courses and get signed up. Stay the course, Caitlyn.*

When I got home, I went straight to my room and closed the door. I wasn't sure if anyone was home or if everyone was out. I didn't really care, either. I grabbed my laptop from my white wooden desk and flopped onto my bed with a heavy sigh.

My heart ached, and tears began to fall. If I were being honest, I wasn't completely sure why I was crying. I guess I wasn't prepared for the reaction from Wyatt. I wanted him to be as excited about it as I was.

I swiped my phone across the monitor on my arm to check my blood sugar: *65 mg/dL.* I slid open the drawer in my nightstand and snatched my glucose tabs. My hand shook as I twisted the cap. I chewed the tablet and let the taste of chocolate marshmallow swish around in my mouth. I swallowed hard before taking a gulp of water from the glass next to my bed.

This was just another reminder of why it wasn't a good idea to get involved with Wyatt as anything more than friends. I hated people seeing me have to take my medicine. I mostly hated the look of pity in their eyes. I sighed and slid the bottle back into the drawer.

Pulling my laptop onto my lap and flipping it open, I sat back on the bed and leaned against my black and white pillows. *Time to do some research.* I Googled *EMT training courses Edenton, NC.* College of The Albemarle was the first entry, so I clicked the link. *Geez, they sure don't make it easy to find.* When I finally got to the *Emergency Medical Science* page, excitement once again coursed through my veins. I filled out the information request form and hit submit.

We shall see what happens.

Chapter 7

Wyatt

I couldn't come up with any reason why Caitlyn left so fast the day before. Had I done something wrong? "Well, buddy. It looks like she's not comin'." A pang shot through my heart as I peered up at the wild horse. "Guess I'll be changin' your bandages by myself."

What did I do wrong? Doesn't she know how excited I am for her to come live on the ranch?

As I changed the horse's dressings, so many scenarios swam around in my head. *Maybe she decided she doesn't want to move out here after all. Maybe having to be my neighbor wasn't somethin' she wanted.* I was hoping once she moved to the ranch, I'd get up enough courage to tell her how I felt. *Maybe bein' more than friends isn't really an option.*

I pulled out my phone.

> *Are ya mad at me? You didn't come help with the horse. Did ya ask your parents about movin' here?*

I saw the three dots appear, and my heart leapt in my chest. But they disappeared quicker than they'd appeared, and my heart sank to the pit of my stomach. Tears formed at the corners of my eyes.

After I was done with the horse's bandages, I decided to take a ride on Flash. Too many emotions were swirling around like a tornado in my brain. I needed to clear my mind, and riding Flash always did that for me. I tacked Flash and climbed into the saddle. Clicking my heels against his body, we trotted out of the stable and into the green grass of the ranch.

I guess I shouldn't have expected her to stick around forever. I mean, my parents didn't, so why would she? I sighed. *At least Colt stayed.*

Before I knew it, I was at my favorite spot, a huge Eastern Redbud tree. It was a gorgeous tree in spring, always the first to bloom with its reddish-purple flowers. But being winter, all I could see was the zigzag of the branches sticking out from the trunk.

I jumped from my perch on Flash to the ground. I fell to my knees beneath the mighty Redbud tree and cried out to God. The tears flowed from my eyes like the Chowan River that I could hear flowing nearby. I lifted my hands to the heavens and tilted my face to the sky.

"God, please don't let Chipmunk walk out of my life. That is much more than I can bear. Give me the strength and the confidence to tell her how I feel. She's my whole heart. I can't lose her, too." I bowed my head and did my best to silence my mind.

Patience, My son. My timing is perfect.

In that moment, peace washed over me like the river water on a hot summer day. I stood from the grass and took a seat back in my saddle. I felt stronger than I had when I'd arrived.

I let Flash run as fast as he wanted back to the stable. I loved the feeling of being on Flash as he sliced through the air. The cool breeze slapped me in the face, but I didn't care. It exhilarated me. The freedom of it.

When I got back to the stable, Colt was standing at the paddock fence watching the wild horse. I rode Flash into the stable and jumped down before removing the saddle and leading him into the corral to cool down. "Good boy, Flash." I patted his neck.

Before getting back to my chores, I joined Colt. "Hey, Colt." I slid my hands into the pockets of my jacket.

"Hey. Good mornin', Wyatt. How are ya?"

"I'm okay." I sighed.

Colt peered over at me. "Your face and that sigh say otherwise. What's goin' on?"

"Caitlyn was supposed to help with the horse this mornin'." I shrugged. "She didn't show up, so I texted her. She didn't respond. She's never not responded before. I don't know what to think of it."

"Yeah. That doesn't sound like her at all." Colt scratched his chin.

"For some reason, things got awkward at the cabins yesterday, and then again last night. I musta done somethin' wrong." I lowered my head and muttered, "Everyone always leaves."

"*I* didn't." Colt huffed.

I sighed. "I know. And I can never tell you how much I appreciate that. And you."

"You just need to tell her how you feel already." Colt slapped his hand on my shoulder and squeezed it.

"I know that, too. Just spent some time with God talkin' 'bout it." I motioned toward the fields.

"Yeah? How'd that go?"

I slid my arms through the fence and rested my elbows on the beam. "Well, He said I need to be patient. Doesn't He know He didn't bless me with that?"

Colt chuckled. "Wyatt, He didn't bless *me* with that, either.

But He'll let ya know when the timin' is right. He did me with Callie."

"He did?"

"Sure did. Believe it or not, that woman turned my insides out the first time I saw her in the Bistro. And somehow, I always knew when she entered a room. I was always stickin' my foot in my mouth whenever I talked to her or was around her." Colt shook and lowered his head.

"Really?" Colt always seemed to have himself together, and he had the looks to go with it. I would have never imagined he had a hard time with Callie.

"Yes. Really. And I know Luke was the same way with Emelia, too. But I think God's still workin' on those two."

"Huh." I bit my bottom lip.

Colt tapped my shoulder. "Things will work out for you in whatever way God intends them to. Just wait and see. But God will let ya know when the right time is to tell Caitlyn how ya feel. Trust Him."

"Thanks, Colt. Guess I'd better get back to my chores."

"Anytime, Wyatt. Anytime. And I mean that."

"I know ya do. Appreciate it." Never had I ever wanted to hug him as much as I did in that moment, but I held it inside and made my way into the stable.

I still wasn't sure how mucking the stalls out was always assigned to me. I shook my head and chuckled. Probably because I was the youngest, and everyone hated that chore. And they knew I'd do it without complaint.

Hopefully, Chipmunk isn't mad at me. I'll have to give her some space. Maybe she's busy getting back to life here. Yeah, she's probably just busy.

I sighed and grabbed the rake to get started. Scooping up the manure, I turned the rake over and let it fall into the wheelbarrow. When the wheelbarrow was full, I pushed it over to the trailer outside. At the end of every week, we took the trailer to the outer parts of the ranch to rot away into the soil.

When I was half done, I checked my watch. *Lunch time.* I leaned the rake against the wall and headed for the house. As I stepped into the kitchen, for the first time since I arrived at Redemption Ranch, the kitchen was deafening silent. I could hear a pin drop.

Where is everyone? I glanced at my watch again. *Am I late?* I brought my watch up to my ear. Tick. Tick. *Still working, so I should be right on time.*

There was a spread of lunch meats, cheeses, and breads on the table that looked like they'd been well picked through. "Everyone ate lunch a little early," Richard stated from behind me. "They wanted to be able to get their chores finished to help with the wild horse."

"Oh." I was a little stunned. "Okay." Those feelings of abandonment engulfed me like a wave crashing onto the shore. In my lifetime, I'd eaten many meals alone. Just never thought I'd have to do that here.

As I was fixing my plate, the kitchen door opened and closed. I peeked over my shoulder to see Jon walking to the sink to wash his hands.

"Hey, Jon."

"Oh hey, Wyatt. Where is everyone?"

"Richard said they all ate already."

"Oh. That's weird."

"Yeah. I guess they want to get chores done to help with the wild horse. That's what Richard told me, anyway."

"That makes sense. I thought maybe I was late." He chuckled.

"I thought I was, too."

Jon and I sat across the table from each other. We weren't as close, as Jon was the same age as Colt. Jon had been chunky like me. But he'd been working out a little over the last year with Spencer, so he had thinned out a bit but wasn't quite as muscular as Colt and Luke. Jon had a great sense of humor, despite having been through so much.

Jon's chair scooting across the hardwood floor transported me back from my thoughts. "I'll see ya at supper, Wyatt," he said.

"Okay. See ya."

Jon slid his plate into the sink and strode out the door.

I shoveled the last bite of my sandwich into my mouth and stood from the table. *Guess I'll have to do the dishes.* Last one out had to do the dishes. It was one of the first rules Colt told me when I arrived.

It didn't take long to get the dishes washed, dried, and put away. I hung the towel up to dry before heading back to the stable. Lunch had always been my source of energy to finish out the afternoon. And it wasn't just the food. It was being surrounded by conversation and people I cared about. And the people who cared about me, especially when no one else seemed to. My family. But today, lunch seemed to drain me.

I grabbed the rake and moved to the next stall.

"Hello, Wyatt."

I froze, and the blood coursing through my veins ran cold. My back was to the stable door, but even though it'd been years since I'd heard that voice, I knew exactly who it belonged to. Slowly turning on my heel toward the voice, I swallowed hard. My tongue clung to the roof of my mouth as if I'd walked a hundred miles through a desert.

"Mom. What are ya doin' here?" I was too stunned that she was actually standing in front of me to be angry.

"I needed to see you." Her hands twisted together in front of her as her voice cracked.

"How did you know where to find me?" My brows furrowed as anger began to bubble from my stomach.

"After all my ideas ran out, I hired a private investigator." She stepped closer, reaching out her hands, before lowering them back to her sides.

I held my palm out toward her. "Don't come any closer. What makes you think I want to see you? And where's Dad?"

"He left me after . . ." Her voice trailed off.

"You left me," I finished for her in a whisper. The words refused to come out any louder.

She lowered her head and cried as she lifted her hand out to touch my cheek. "Baby, I'm so sorry."

I pulled my head back out of her reach. "Sorry doesn't really cut it, Mom. You left me! Alone! I had no one! I was thirteen years old!" I screamed at her as tears stung my eyes.

She cast her eyes down at her hands. "I know. I don't want to upset you."

"Then, why did you come here? Did ya really think I'd be happy to see ya?"

"I don't know." She breathed deep. "Look, I'm staying at the Sunset Motel for at least the next few days if you want to talk. Room 136."

"I won't," I said through clenched teeth.

"Okay." She turned and disappeared out the door just as she had done six years before.

Only after she was out of sight did I take a deep breath. My chest heaved as ragged breaths tried desperately to fill my lungs. *What is she doin' here?* I stared at the door as if she would reappear, just like I'd done for so long after she and Dad had left.

As I was turning around to get back to work, I noticed a white envelope on the table next to the door. I rushed over and snatched it from its resting place. My hands were ready to rip it up, but my heart hesitated. I grunted as I folded it and jammed it into my back pocket before going back to finish my chore.

When I was done, it wasn't quite supper time, so I thought I would call Caitlyn. I walked out the back door of the stable and found Colt working on a piece of the corral fence. "Hey, Colt. Need a hand?" I asked as I pushed my phone back into my pocket.

His eyes lifted to me. "Yeah. Couldn't hurt. Just hold this piece right here. Thanks."

"No problem." I took hold of the log and moved it back into place. "So, you'll never believe who just showed up here."

"Oh, who's that?"

"My mother."

Colt almost dropped the post he was trying to attach to the log. "You're kiddin' me? What did she want after all these years?"

I scratched the back of my head after we had the fencing in place. "I'm not sure, but she left an envelope."

After making sure the post was secure, Colt wiped his brow as he stood straight. "What's in it?"

"Dunno." I shrugged. "Haven't opened it yet."

"Are ya goin' to?"

"Not sure."

"Don't ya wanna know?"

"I think she and my dad made it very clear how they felt about me when they left me." Tears pricked my eyes again.

"Well, at least think about it before you throw it away."

I sighed. "I will."

Get rid of all bitterness, rage, and anger . . . Be kind and

compassionate . . . Forgiving each other just as I have forgiven you.

I closed my eyes and lifted my face. *I'll try. I promise.*

Chapter 8

Caitlyn

I left the administration building of the College of The Albemarle with a renewed feeling of hope about my future. I lifted my face to the late afternoon sun that managed to take a bit of the chill out of the air. I had filled out the admissions application with a counselor, and she said all I needed to do was add the school to my FAFSA I'd already completed. The only other thing I needed to do was complete a 200–300-word essay on why I wanted to be in the program. *That will be easy enough.*

I bounced happily to my car. My heart was full of thoughts about what my future might hold. *I can't wait to tell Cowboy.* My heart plummeted at the thought. What if he was just as excited about any aspect of my life as he was about my move to the ranch? I didn't think I could handle that again. As much as I wanted to drive straight to the ranch and find out, I drove home instead. *I should get started on my essay anyway.*

As I was pulling up to my house, I noticed Wyatt's big black Dodge Ram parked in front. I stepped out on the sidewalk and caught a glimpse of him on the porch. Something was wrong. It was written all over his face. I hurried up the steps to the front porch where he was sitting on the bench next to the front door.

"What's wrong?" I dropped down next to him on the

whitewashed wooden bench.

Wyatt shook his head and gulped. "Well, first, you didn't text me back when I texted you. You always text back," he muttered.

My eyes bulged. "I'm so sorry, Cowboy." I placed my hand on his arm. A spark of heat hit my palm. "I was working on getting into my EMT classes, and then, I fell asleep. I'm so sorry."

"I'm glad to know you're not mad at me." Gladness was not reflected on his face, though. He never lifted his eyes to meet mine.

"What else is botherin' ya? I see it on your face." He never was good at hiding how he was feeling, even if he did not express it.

"My mom showed up at the ranch this mornin'."

"What?" I leaned against the back of the bench.

"Yeah, she said my dad left her right after they left me." His eyes remained on a white envelope with his name scrawled on the front as he twirled it in his hands. "She said she hired a private investigator to find me."

I bit my bottom lip and pointed to the envelope. "What's that?"

"She left it in the stable." He held it up in the air.

"Are ya gonna open it?"

He shrugged. "I dunno. To be honest, I don't really want to know or read anythin' she has to say."

"Don't ya wanna know why she's here?"

"Honestly . . ." He sighed. "I don't really care. I tried tearin' it up, but I couldn't bring myself to do it."

I flung my arms around his neck. In that moment, I didn't know what to say. Just that I needed to be close to him. And for him to know that he was cared about. He didn't need more empty words.

When Wyatt's arms wrapped around me, warmth engulfed me. *Will I always let my fear overpower my desire to tell him how I really feel? I guess I'll just take the moments as they come.* I held on a little tighter. A little longer.

"Thank you," he whispered in my ear.

"For what?" I asked as he ended our hug, taking his warmth with him.

"For always bein' here for me. Your friendship means more to me than you know." He took my hand in his.

"I feel the same way about you." My heart swam in his glassy eyes. Hope sprang inside me. Was he about to tell me something I'd wanted to hear for so long?

"Chipmunk, I—"

At the sound of the door opening, Wyatt withdrew his hand from mine.

"There ya are," Dyl said. "Mom's been lookin' for ya."

Dyl! Not again! I sighed and held up my index finger. "Okay. I'll be in. Give me a minute."

"It's okay. I should get back to the ranch." Wyatt stood and shoved the envelope into his pocket. "I'll talk to ya later."

"Sorry, Sis. I didn't mean to interrupt anythin'."

I slapped my hands on my knees before rising from the bench. "It's okay."

Dyl wrapped his arm around my neck and escorted me inside. We found Mom and Dad in the kitchen.

"Hey, Mom. Hey, Dad. Dyl said you were lookin' for me?"

"We just wanted to check in and see what you've been up to." Mom sat at the island in the middle of our kitchen, her arms resting on the marble countertop.

"Well, I went to the College of The Albemarle to see about their EMT classes. I just have a couple of things I need to do before they can admit me into the program." I smiled. "Classes won't start until mid-January."

"That's awesome." Dad patted my shoulder. "We're so proud of you, honey."

"I'm excited to get started. I hope I get accepted. At least I have the whole Christmas season to relax and prepare. After I submit the essay they require, that is."

Mom smiled and said, "I have no doubt you will get in. You always succeed at everthin' you put your mind to."

Not everything.

"So, what did Wyatt want? He sat out on the porch for quite a while. I tried to get him to come in but . . ." Mom shrugged.

"He just needed someone to talk to about somethin'. Not really my place to say."

"Okay. I'm sure glad you both have each other."

"Me, too."

"Have you checked your sugar lately?" Mom asked.

Always the worrier. I rolled my eyes and lifted my phone to my arm. When it beeped, I turned my phone to her.

"Thank you." She smiled.

"You're welcome. Um. There *is* somethin' I wanted to talk to you about." *What are you doin'? You said ya weren't gonna ask.* "I wanted to see what you both thought about me movin' to the ranch. I asked Uncle Colt, and he said it's okay with him if it's okay with both of you." I bit my bottom lip. Hard.

"What? You just got back home, and you want to leave us again?" Tears filled Mom's eyes and voice.

"It's only across town. Kind of. Will you just think about it?" I pleaded.

Dad wrapped his arm around Mom's shoulders. "We'll think about it and let you know what we decide. Mom was lookin' for ya because we wanted to see if you'd be able to take a shift. Maggie needs to take the day off."

"Sure, I can do that. I can go back to work at the café if ya want or need me to." I was willing to do anything to increase my chances of them saying yes.

"Thanks, sweetie." Mom rested her hand on top of mine. "We'd love that. I think everyone would love to see you there again."

"Okay. Well, I'm gonna head up to bed. Love you. See ya in the mornin'.'"

"Night, Sis. Love you, too," Dad said to my retreating back.

I ascended the stairs to my room and closed the door. I didn't mean to ask about moving to the ranch, but I opened my mouth, and the words spewed out. *It's too late now. Guess I'll just have to wait and see what they say.* I realized that I was eighteen and could just move there with Uncle Colt's permission, but I respected my parents too much to make that kind of decision without them. I was *barely* eighteen.

I wanted to at least start my essay, so I pulled my laptop onto my lap from my bedside table. I wrote about how I'd always wanted to be a nurse since I was diagnosed with diabetes. Then, I wrote about what happened to Quinn.

Once I hit 300 words, I felt my essay was complete. I could have written more, but I didn't want to go against the requirements. It might have affected whether they admitted me or not. I couldn't take that chance. I sent it off to the email address of the admissions counselor, Mrs. Wiggins.

After I added the school to my FAFSA, I put on my pajamas and slid under the covers of my bed. I stared at the wallpaper on my phone. It was a selfie Wyatt and I had taken at the Kickoff to Christmas Festival. I brought my fingers to my lips before pressing them to my phone, over his face. He wasn't in the best mood when he left my house. I hoped he would be okay. His mom showing up must have really wrecked him.

I took a last look at the picture. "Goodnight, Cowboy." I set my phone on the table and knew my dreams would be filled with him.

Chapter 9

Wyatt

Standing on my porch and facing my door, I stared at the envelope. My heart wanted to rip it open and drink in every word like it was ice-cold water on a hot summer day. But my mind argued that Mom didn't deserve it.

I sighed, turned the knob, and stepped inside. I tossed the keys and the letter in a small bowl I kept on top of the wooden shelf I'd made in wood shop class my junior year of high school. Next to the bowl was the unfinished, half-carved horse I'd been trying to work on for far too long. It was supposed to be a Christmas present. *Suppose I'd best work on that tomorrow. Or else it might never get done.*

Mentally, the day had taken a toll on me. I covered my yawn with my arm. I slipped off my boots and left them by the door before shuffling to my room and collapsing on my bed.

* * *

The next morning, I woke up with a renewed sense of hope. It was amazing how you felt when you got a full night's rest. I stretched my entire body and rolled out of bed.

After I showered, I stuffed my feet in my boots, flopped my hat on top of my head, and made my way to the paddock to check on the horse and change his bandages. The horse was running along the fence. *Well, it looks like his leg is finally feelin' better.*

"Hey, boy. You must be feelin' better," I greeted him when I stepped up to the fence.

At the sound of my voice, he stopped running and trotted over to me.

"Good mornin', Wyatt. How are ya?" Colt asked as he approached the paddock, his hands full with salve and bandages.

"Oh, I'm doin' all right." *Well, I guess that takes care of that.*

"Make any decisions about ya mom?"

I massaged the back of my neck and sighed. "No. I haven't even opened the envelope. I've tried to tear it up a couple of times, but for some reason, I can't seem to do it."

Colt removed the bandages from the horse's hindquarters. "Maybe deep down ya really want to know what she has to say. Maybe it will be closure for ya."

"Yeah, maybe so."

"Think ya could help me? He doesn't seem to hold still for anyone the way he does for you. Kinda reminds me of Callie and Warrior."

"Sure." I strolled around to the gate and stepped inside the paddock. I moved slowly toward the horse. "Hey, boy. Colt just wants to help you feel better."

I rested a hand on each side of the horse's face, and the fear disappeared from his eyes. Not sure what replaced it. Peace, maybe? I wished we could have kept him, but I knew that wasn't what was best for him.

When Colt finished changing the bandages, he picked up the jar of salve and the used bandages. "Thanks for the help."

"Sure. No problem," I replied to his back. I turned back to

the horse. "Guess I'd better get started on my chores. See ya later, buddy. Be good." I patted his face before heading to the stable.

After letting the horses out into the corral, I shuffled back inside and grabbed a shovel and rake from their hangers on the wall.

"Mornin', Wyatt."

That same feeling of dread I'd felt the first time I'd heard her voice again coursed through my entire body. I closed my eyes, sighed, and turned around. Through clenched teeth, I said, "Mom, you really can't keep showin' up here."

"I'm sorry, but I would like to talk with you. Did you read my letter?" Hope filled her eyes.

"No. Not yet."

The hope disappeared as she sighed. "I'm here because I'm in recovery. I'm doin' the steps. I'm on step nine, makin' amends."

"So, you came for your own benefit then."

"No. That's not true at all. I've been sober for almost a year. I've been searchin' for you with every resource I could find ever since. It breaks my heart what I've put you through. I know I don't deserve your forgiveness, but would ya at least think about it?" Even if her words hadn't been filled with pleading, her big, light brown eyes sure were.

I sighed as my heart softened . . . a little. "I'll think about it. I promise. Now, can I get back to my chores?"

A huge smile spread across her face. "That's all I can ask." She turned to go before partially turning back around. "I hope I see you soon."

"Okay," was all I could manage to say. I wasn't sure *what* to say.

Once she was gone, the tear that had been hiding inside the

corner of my eye fell onto my cheek and ran down onto my shirt. I swiped the remnants of the tear from my cheek and dug the shovel hard into the pile of hay and manure. *Why did she have to come here and bring up feelings I buried a long time ago?*

With each jab into the hay, I felt my anger lessen. By the time I was done, my emotions were back in check. I pulled out my phone: 5:00 p.m. *Shoot! I lost track of time. Worked right through lunch.* My stomach gurgled in response. *Looks like it's time for supper. I'll put the horses back in their stalls after I eat.*

After hanging the shovel and rake back on the wall, I slid my hands from my gloves and laid them in the toolbox drawer just beside where the rake and shovel were hanging. My footsteps were heavy, like my heart, as I plodded to the house. I couldn't wait to see what Richard had made for supper. My mouth watered at the thought.

I was so emotionally and physically drained that it took everything I had in me not to turn toward my cabin, shower, and hit the hay. My stomach growled, and I remembered why I hadn't. And being around people who actually cared about me and wanted me . . . well, that was something I needed, too. Much more than food or sleep.

The kitchen was alive again as it usually was. It was unlike lunch the day before. I hoped the kitchen would never be that quiet or empty again.

"Hey, Wyatt," everyone greeted as I shuffled over to the sink to wash my hands.

"Hey. Somethin' wrong?" Luke asked as he pumped some soap into his hands.

"No. Why?" I rinsed my hands under the hot water.

"You've been standin' at the sink longer than it usually

takes to wash ya hands. Twice."

I shook my head. "Oh. Sorry."

"So, what's up?"

Since he wasn't the first person to notice, I guess I'd been wearing my emotions on the outside. "My mom stopped by the other day. And today."

Luke's mouth fell open. "What?"

"Yeah. She says she's been sober for a year."

"Guys, wanna come join us at the table so we can eat, please?" Colt interrupted.

"Oh. Yeah. Sorry." I glanced over my shoulder and dried my hands on my pants before taking my place at the table.

I peered across the table as Luke lipped, "We'll talk later."

I nodded as we joined hands in prayer.

"Lord, we thank you for these gifts," Colt began. "For the food on the table and the people around it. Use this food to the nourishment of our bodies, so we can continue to do Your will. Let our lives be Your will and not our own. Amen."

"Amen," we all responded at the same time.

"Let's eat!" Colt called out.

Different conversations began as Colt passed fried chicken and then mashed potatoes to Callie to his left. Everyone was there: Colt, Callie, Emelia, Luke, Spencer, Richard, and Jon.

I ate in silence as I usually did. I wasn't really sure, but that day, I didn't have much to say anyway. My mind was too full of my mother's second surprise visit to handle any of the small talk.

After I finished, I set my dishes in the sink and headed out to the corral to put the horses back in their stalls. "Hey, Wyatt! Wait up!" Luke hollered from behind. I turned to see him jogging toward me. As he fell in step beside me, he asked, "What's goin' on?"

I shrugged. "My mom just showed up here out of nowhere. Twice."

"That's rough, man." He put his arm around my shoulders and squeezed. "So, what are ya gonna do?"

"I'm not sure. Part of me wants to know why she's here, but the other part of me feels like she made her decision when she and my dad left me for drugs."

"Maybe you could give her a chance to say what she needs to say and then make a choice."

"Yeah. Maybe." I massaged the back of my neck. "She wrote me a letter."

"Oh. I'm guessin' you're tryin' to decide whether to read it or not?"

"Yeah." I pulled gently on the rope attached to Flash and led him toward the stable.

Luke followed with Minnie. Majesty snorted. "I'll be right back for ya, Majesty. Don't get jealous." He chuckled before returning his attention to me. "Do ya think you'll read it?"

"Caitlyn thinks I should. So does Colt." I shrugged.

"I have to say that I agree with them. You'll never know what's in her heart unless ya read it."

"You're all probably right, but I'm not sure I'm ready." My voice cracked.

"Well, if ya ever need or want to talk about it, you know I'm always here." Luke patted me on the back.

"Thanks, Luke. And thanks for the help with the horses," I said as I closed the door to Flash's stall.

"No problem."

We brought the rest of the horses into the stable two by two in silence. As Luke closed the door to the final stall—Tinkerbell's—he said, "Have a good night, Wyatt."

"Good night. And thanks, again," I turned from the stall to

find myself alone. I sighed deeply.

As I sauntered home, my mind and heart were at war with each other. My heart wanted to read the letter from Mom; my brain was completely against it. The little boy deep inside me wanted to run to the motel and fall into her arms and forgive her for everything she had ever done to me.

My back stiffened. *Ya don't owe her anythin', Wyatt. She's the one who owes you.*

I shook the thoughts out of my mind and stepped inside my cabin. Throwing my keys in the bowl, the letter beckoned to me. I grunted and shuffled to the bathroom to take a shower and, hopefully, drown out all the thoughts of Mom.

After putting on my pajamas, I couldn't ignore the nagging of my heart anymore, so I went back to the shelf and grabbed the letter. I stared at my name on the front as I made my way back to my room. I lay down on my bed as I ripped open the envelope before I had any second thoughts.

My Dearest Wyatt,

I struggled to move my eyes past my name. I always did love Mom's whimsical handwriting. The way she curled the first part of her letters.

I'm so sorry for everything your dad and I have put you through.

After your dad left me, I went back for you, but you weren't there. I'm not really sure why I thought you would be.

Did she really think I was still there? I wondered. *Just waiting idly by for them to come back for me?*

I love you. I always have and always will.

Funny way of showin' it. I scoffed.

Soon after your dad left me, I found out he overdosed. I'm sorry to tell you this in a letter. I really wanted to tell you in person, but he died that night.

What? Tears formed in my eyes. *He's dead?* Anger surged through my entire body. *How could they take time away from me? How could someone not tell me?*

I crumpled the letter into a ball and threw it across the room. It bounced off the wall and rolled under a small table in the corner. With clenched fists, I rose from my bed and stomped to the living room, grabbed the half-completed wooden horse, along with my knife, and went to sit on the porch.

Wood carving had always soothed my soul. One of the homeless men who watched out for me had taught me how to do it. It ended up being one of the ways I'd been able to make some money when I was in Texas. It wasn't a lot, but it was enough for me to get food each day.

That horse was special, though. It was a Christmas present. For Emelia. I was doing my best to get it just right. I had to get it right. It was a replica of Tinkerbell with little cowgirl boots in her mouth. Once I finished carving it out, I was going to paint it to match Tinkerbell's coat, and the boots would be pink. I hoped Emelia was going to stay at least for Christmas. But no one really knew for sure what she was going to do.

I hoped she stayed. For herself. For Luke. He was all in where she was concerned. I couldn't imagine what it'd do to him if she left. Would he leave, too?

My mom's face floated through my mind. *Why'd she have to come here? I wish she would've just stayed away.*

My heart ached just like it did the day I found out they'd left me. It was a stabbing pain, like a double-edged knife digging deep, trying to do as much damage as possible with each jab. I squeezed the piece of wood so hard my knuckles turned white. I raised my arm to chuck the wood as far as I could throw it, but I lowered it just as quickly because it was a gift, and that was more important than any of my pain. It had to be.

As I carved the finishing touches on the horse, I noticed the moon was high in the sky. I yawned. I was emotionally and physically spent.

As I rose from my chair, I folded up my knife and pushed it into the pocket of my plaid pajama pants before shuffling inside. Stifling another yawn, I sprawled out on my bed.

Chapter 10

Caitlyn

As I meandered around the feed store, which was also the local western wear store, I wondered what to get Wyatt for Christmas. I was running out of time. I ran my hand over a couple of silver belt buckles with horses on them. *He has plenty of buckles. Seems like he wears a different one every day of the week.*

Walking further down the aisle, I bit my lip as I pondered the possibilities. When I reached the wall of hats, my eyes lit up like a Christmas tree. Wyatt *did* mention once how he needed a new hat to wear. I picked up a black felt hat. It had a curved brim and what was called a cattleman crease along the length of the top. There was also a brown and tan braided band around the crown. *This is the one.*

I opened my phone to check the time. *Oh, I'd better get checked out and get over to the café for my shift.*

After checking out, I laid the hat box in my car's trunk before slipping inside and driving to the café. Since the café wasn't that far, I thought about walking, but I didn't want Wyatt to see my car parked in front of the store. I was afraid he might figure it out, and I didn't want to take the chance of ruining the surprise.

Parked in front of the café, I sat in silence. I felt as if my life had taken a huge step backward. In a way, I suppose it had, but I couldn't start classes until after the first of the year. December would be a season of rest and healing. Things I needed so much.

Thank you, God, for this season of my life. I know I'm where I'm supposed to be, but sometimes, I just need You more. Warmth spread through me; comfort and peace followed. "Thank you, Lord," I whispered.

"There's my girl!" Mom exclaimed as I walked through the front door.

Blood rushed to my cheeks. "Um. Hi, Mom."

"Welcome home," Mr. Windham said, raising his to-go bag in my direction on his way out, no doubt holding his usual chicken salad sandwich and a bag of plain Lay's potato chips.

"Thank you." I smiled warmly as I glanced up into his gray eyes encircled by wrinkles, resulting from his friendly smile. I put my things behind the counter and tied my apron around my waist. "Where do ya want me to start, Mom?"

"First, with a hug." She held out her arms to me.

Rolling my eyes, I fell into her arms and wrapped mine around her. I breathed deeply. There was no better place than in the middle of my mother's embrace. I'd missed it more than anyone could ever know. The only thing that came close was Wyatt's hugs.

"Now, you can go back and work on the dishes." Mom patted my back, amusement dancing in her eyes. She knew how much I loathed doing dishes.

I groaned. "Ugh. Really?"

"Really. Now, go." She nudged me in the direction of the kitchen. "Later, you can help me with the cake for the Reynold's wedding this weekend."

"Oh, yay!" I happily bounced to the back of the kitchen.

As I slipped my hands into the sudsy sink pool, my mind wandered. Making cakes was my favorite thing to do at the café. Especially piping the borders and making the flowers out of fondant. With my mom. And when Dad got involved, you can bet there was a huge mess and some funny antics. That's why he usually left the baking to us. Don't get me wrong, there were some things he made deliciously well, but it usually looked like a bomb went off in the kitchen. I always wished Dyl would help with the baking. He used to when he was younger. But now, he was busy with baseball—his first love. I couldn't blame him for that. He had big dreams. And I had no doubt he'd reach them.

As I dried a plate and put it away, my hand began to tremble, and a bead of sweat trickled down the side of my cheek. I grabbed my phone as the alarm began to sound, alerting me that my blood sugar was off. I scanned the monitor on my arm. When it beeped, I glanced down. *Sixty-five.* My vision went blurry.

"Mom!" I leaned against the counter.

"What's wrong?" Mom came rushing in.

"My sugar is too low."

She wrapped her arms around me. "Let's get you sitting down before you fall." We walked carefully to her office to the left of the kitchen, and she helped me sit at her desk. "Stay right there."

I hated the feeling of low blood sugar. High blood sugar, too. I knew God had a bigger plan. I needed to lean into *His* understanding and not my own. Easier said than done, though. My arms felt like twenty-pound weights as I lifted them to rest on the desk. My head spun, and I lay my head on my arms.

"Here, sweetheart." One hand set the glass of orange juice on the table, and one caressed my back. "Drink this while I make you a PB and J."

"Thanks, Mom." I flashed her a weak smile before picking up the glass and taking a drink. As I drank the juice, I let out a sigh of relief as my hands became less shaky with every swig.

"Here's your sandwich. Juice helping at all?" Mom's voice was laced with concern as she slid the plate across the desk.

"Yeah."

"Okay. If you need me, I'll be up front."

"Thank you."

When she disappeared out of the office, I deeply inhaled. Those episodes always zapped me of my energy. Mentally *and* physically. Sometimes, I felt it drained me more mentally than anything else.

I finished my juice and sandwich in silence. Soaking in the solitude, I was grateful no one else had been around. I didn't want anyone to ever see me like that. Ever. Outside of my family, that is. I barely wanted *them* to see me. But especially Wyatt.

Once I'd felt my body come back to some sense of normalcy, I cautiously stood from the chair. I steadied myself and slowly went back to the sink. I put in more soap and warmed up the water. I didn't want to finish the dishes, and I knew Mom wouldn't have made me, but I always finished the job I started. These episodes of low blood sugar exhausted me, so all I really wanted to do was go home and crawl into bed.

"What are you doin'?" Mom entered the kitchen and asked as I laid a dish in the sanitizing sink after rinsing it off in the sink containing just hot water.

"I'm finishing the job you asked me to do." I glanced in her direction before dipping my hands back into the hot, soapy water.

"Dyl finished practice early and said he would take over

for you. He'll be here shortly. You need to go home and rest." She pulled my hands from the water and dried them on the towel she always had hanging from her apron.

"Ya sure?" My eyes met hers.

"Yes. Now, go." She pointed toward the door.

"Yes, ma'am." I wrapped my arms around her middle and squeezed. "I love you."

"I love you, too." She squeezed me back. "Now, go before I have to fire you." She chuckled. It was a wonderful sound. I had missed that, too.

I held up my hands and laughed. "Okay. Okay. I'm goin'."

Chapter 11

Wyatt

I stood at the door of the Sunset Motel, staring at number 136 for what seemed like forever. After willing my fist to raise to the wood, I knocked three times.

A few seconds later, a bang emitted from the room. It sounded like maybe a lamp had been knocked over. The door crept open, and my bleary-eyed mother appeared, arching her neck up at me. At five-foot-nine, I towered over her five-foot-two frame. Her eyes grew large. She swiped her eyes with the back of her hand. "Wyatt, you came."

"I'm not sure what I'm doin' here." My jaw clenched. *Is she usin' again? If she is, is it my fault?* An ache rose in my chest at the thought.

Mom opened the door wider. "Do ya wanna come in?"

I shoved my hands in my pockets and stepped over the threshold into the dingy, dark room. Mom closed the door and flipped the light switch. The standing floor lamp behind an ugly green recliner lit up.

"You usin' again?" I asked before my brain even thought about it.

"No, son."

My jaw clenched tighter. "Don't call me son. I stopped bein' your son a long time ago."

She lowered her head and raised her hand to her eyes. "I deserve that. But no, I'm not usin' again, and I won't ever. I've lost too much to that stuff already. I was sleepin'. I've been havin' trouble sleepin' at night, so I sleep when I can." Mom cleaned off the chair that had a pile of clothes on it. "Sorry. I need to do laundry. You can sit down if you wanna."

I lowered myself into the chair and rested my elbows on my knees. "So, what're ya doin' here?"

"I told ya. I've been lookin' for ya since right after we left."

"Then why did ya leave in the first place?" My voice cracked with hurt that I thought was long dead and buried.

"Because your dad told me to. And I didn't know we were leavin' for good. Eventually, I thought you'd be better off without us." Her gaze moved to her interlaced fingers lying in her lap.

"I was a child! How could I have been better off, Mom? Huh? How?" My voice rang out in the air as my mouth foamed with anger. "I lived in a bus station! I ate people's leftover food! Luckily, I was in the right place at the right time and ended up here. Colt gave me everythin' you and Dad were supposed to . . . but didn't."

Tears dripped from Mom's eyes. "Can you ever forgive me?"

God, help me. "Honestly? I'm not sure. But I'm willin' ta try. That's what God wants me to do."

"That's all I can ask."

"How long are ya plannin' on bein' in town?" I rose from the chair as the air became humid, and it became harder to breathe in the confines of the small room.

"I'll be here for as long as it takes."

I wasn't entirely sure what that meant, but I nodded and

placed my hand on the doorknob. "I'll come back again sometime."

"Okay," she said faintly. She cleared her throat. "Thank you for comin'."

"Sure." I swung open the door and stomped my feet on the other side. I let the door click behind me before taking a deep breath.

As I trudged back to my truck, my thoughts went to Caitlyn. *I need to see her.* Yeah, that girl had my whole heart. I just needed to tell her that. No matter the moment—good or bad—I wanted and needed her to know it.

As I pulled up to the dark teal house with the wrap-around porch, I finally released the breath I felt like I'd been holding in. My footsteps were heavy as I lifted them on each step. At the door, I rapped my knuckles against it but didn't feel them connect with it.

"Hey, Wyatt," Mr. Logan said.

"Hi, Mr. Logan. Is Caitlyn home?" I tucked my fingers into my pockets and my thumbs through the belt loops.

"She's sleeping. She had an episode at work earlier."

My heart dropped to my stomach. "What? Is she okay?"

"I'm awake, Dad." Caitlyn appeared behind him.

Relief flooded my entire body. She looked so fragile. I couldn't explain it really.

Caitlyn stepped outside onto the porch, and we sat on the bench that held so many of our memories. The flowers bloomed behind us. They were bright yellow. I think Caitlyn told me once they were Winter Jasmine. It seemed like a waste of a flower because they had no scent. Her mom had big planters on either side of the bottom of the steps. Both had white flowers, which Mrs. Logan had mentioned were Christmas Roses. I thought it was funny because they didn't look like roses at all. And they didn't smell like them either.

Caitlyn stared into my eyes. "What's wrong?"

I laid my hands on her forearms as we faced each other. "First of all, how are you? What happened?"

"I'm fine. My blood sugar just got kinda low." She shrugged. "It always zaps my energy, so Mom made me come home. She actually threatened to fire me."

"What?" I chuckled. That sounded just like Mrs. Logan to do something like that.

"Yeah. Of course, she was just kiddn'. She can't afford to fire me." She giggled.

"Would it be okay if I gave you a hug?" I asked quietly.

"Yes, I could definitely use one of your hugs."

I wrapped my arms around her, and she melted into my chest. Lying my chin on the top of her head, I sighed contentedly. That was where I wanted her to be forever. Nestled in the safety of my arms just like she was in my heart and my life. I'd have done anything in my power to keep her safe and secure.

When she left my arms, Caitlyn took her warmth and comfort with her. "So, it's your turn. What's wrong?"

"Um." I played with the button on the sleeve of my flannel shirt. "I just left from seein' my mom."

"You did? How'd it go?"

"She asked me to forgive her for leavin' me. But how do I do that?"

"What did you tell her?"

"I told her I'd try because that's what God wants me to do. She said that's all she can ask of me. Told her I might come back sometime. Then, I left."

"Oh, Cowboy." Caitlyn lifted her hand to my cheek.

My skin sizzled as she grazed her thumb along my upper cheek. I leaned into her hand and closed my eyes, finding so much comfort in the contact.

"I'm okay, Chipmunk. I promise." I placed my hand on top of hers. But I avoided her eyes. If she looked into mine, she'd see every emotion her mere presence evoked. Everything I ever felt for her.

"Ya sure?"

I nodded.

"Okay."

"I'd better let ya rest. I just . . . I just needed to see ya."

"Anytime. I'll always be here for you. You know that." Her voice was so tender and sweet.

God, I love her.

We stood from the bench.

"Thank you. You know that means the world to me." I pulled her closer. I wanted more than anything to kiss her lips, but I lowered my lips to her forehead. I closed my eyes and breathed in the scent of her hair—always the sweet scent of strawberries. "Good night and sweet dreams, Chipmunk."

"Good night and sweet dreams, Cowboy."

I watched her walk inside like I always did before turning to leave.

* * *

I knocked on the door of the cabin that belonged to Emelia. She slowly opened the door. "Hey, Wyatt."

My heart ached at the sound of her hollow voice and the sight of the dark circles under her eyes. "Uh, hey, Emelia." I ran my fingers over the hairs at the nape of my neck. "Are ya busy?" I wasn't entirely sure why I was so nervous, but my stomach was twisted into a pretzel.

"No. Not really. What's up?" She leaned against the door jamb.

"Well, I'm runnin' out of time. I want to get Chip— Caitlyn somethin' special for Christmas. I have an idea, but I'm not sure if it would be special enough for her."

Emelia's eyes lit up a little bit. "Let me get my jacket."

Yes! Emelia knew Caitlyn pretty well, and she was a girl . . . well, a woman.

As we sat in my truck on the way to town, Emelia asked, "So, what thoughts have you had about what to get her?"

None. Absolutely none. But I couldn't tell her that. "Do *you* have any ideas?"

"Hmm. What about a necklace or earrings? I don't know a single woman who doesn't love getting jewelry."

I shrugged. I had no idea what a woman likes to get.

"Well, let's head to the store and see what they have. We can always decide on something else if nothing catches your eye."

I nodded. "Okay. That works. But it has to be the perfect thing."

When we arrived at Max's Jewels, I held my breath as I opened the door for Emelia.

"Thank you."

Here goes nothin'.

The door chimed, and a voice bellowed from the back of the store, "Be right with ya."

Max was a big, burly guy who you'd think would be found in a biker bar, not a jewelry store. The store was decorated in different shades of brown and gold. Gold trim surrounded the glass that encased the different pieces of jewelry on display. Large chandeliers hung from the ceiling.

When Max appeared in the doorway, he said, "Oh, hey there, Wyatt. Emelia."

"Hey, Max. How are ya?"

"I'm good. Can't complain. What can I do for ya today?"

"I'm lookin' for a special gift." Heat radiated up my neck and into my cheeks.

"Do you know what kind?"

My shoulders scrunched against my neck. "Maybe a necklace?"

"Okay. Do you know what kind of stones you want? Gold or silver chain?"

My shoulders bobbed again. I had a feeling my shoulders were going to hurt from shrugging so much.

"Well, what's her birthstone?"

"I have no idea. Her birthday is in December, like mine."

"That would be a topaz." Max reached down and unlocked one of the display cases in front of us. "That would be this color here."

Nothing jumped out at me. "Her favorite color is pink. Is there a stone that's pink?"

"Yes, there is. Let's go over here to this display." He held his hand out toward another case across the room. "I have a necklace that I just got in last week." He removed it from the glass enclosure before I could lay my eyes on it. Max glided it across his palm and let the necklace rest in the center of it.

My breath caught in my throat. It was a silver snowflake with pink and white stones at the points. The white stones were in the middle of the shapes that looked like leaves. The snowflake was attached to a thin silver chain.

I glanced over at Emelia. My eyes felt as big as saucers. "What do ya think? I think I like this one."

"It's beautiful, Wyatt. I know she'll love it." She smiled brighter than I'd seen her do in what seemed like such a long time.

I pointed at Max's hand. "This is the one. How much is it?"

"With tax," he pounded the numbers into his calculator, "it'll be $193.72."

"I'll take it." I pulled my wallet from my back pocket and slid my debit card from its slot before holding it out to him. My heart was giddy with excitement. I couldn't wait to give the necklace to Caitlyn. I hoped I could hold out until Christmas.

"Excellent. I'll ring it up and put it in a gift bag for ya."

I nodded as Max went to the register.

"I'm so excited for you, Wyatt," Emelia said. "She really is going to love it."

"I can't wait to see her face when she opens it." I smiled down at her.

"I just need ya to sign." Max placed the receipt and pen in front of me as he held up a small silver bag with red and green tissue paper sticking out of the top.

I scribbled my name across the line, and Max held the bag out to me. "Thank you for your business. I hope she loves it."

"Thank you." I looped my finger through the string handles and rushed out the door. "Now, I just have to keep it a secret and not give it to her too soon."

Emelia laughed. "Secrets aren't my strong suit, either."

"I guess we can get back to the ranch. Should be just in time for supper."

"Thank you for inviting me, Wyatt. I didn't realize how much I needed it. I'm tired of people walking around like I'm going to break. I have appreciated that you don't do that. So, thank you for that, too."

"Everyone just loves you. And thank you for comin' with me for support and your opinion and idea."

"Of course."

"So . . . I could use some advice."

"Sure. What can I help with?" Emelia twisted in the seat to

face me.

"Well, my mom showed up on the ranch a few days ago. She wants me to forgive her for leaving me. I want to, but I don't really know how." I sighed.

"Yeah . . ." She ran her hands down her thighs. "I struggle with forgiveness, too. I know God wants me to forgive Gary, but I'm just not ready. One day, I hope I can forgive him. For me."

"I'm not sure I'm ready, either."

Emelia laid her hand on my forearm, which was resting on the center console. "And that's okay, Wyatt. I'm still learning about my relationship with God, but I know He would want your forgiveness to be sincere and not just superficial and lip service."

"Thank you. My heart and my mind just can't seem to get on the same page. My heart wants to forgive her for the little boy I used to be, but my brain sends off alarm bells every time she is near me."

"That's understandable. You went through a lot because of what she did. All we can do is pray and ask God to guide us in the direction He wants us to go." She grabbed hold of my hand. "Father God, we ask that You work in our hearts and help us to forgive those who have wronged us. Help us to rid our minds and hearts of the bitterness housed there. We love you, Lord. We praise You and honor You. Amen."

"Amen."

"Sorry I'm not better at that."

"Don't be sorry. It was heartfelt and so needed. Thank you for praying for me. And for you."

After pulling up to the main house for supper, we strode inside to join the others. I had no doubt they were all seated around the old wood table.

Chapter 12

Caitlyn

I knocked on Wyatt's door, hoping I was early enough to catch him before he got started on his chores. Uncle Colt said I could steal him away for a little while. The door crept open, and behind it was a sleepy-eyed, tousle-haired Wyatt.

A sheepish grin appeared across my face. "Mornin'. It's the week before Christmas, and we haven't picked a tree to plant yet," I reminded him. "Or gotten pinwheels done."

He ran his hand through his hair. "Oh. I totally forgot."

"Well, get dressed, and let's go." I bounced up and down.

Wyatt chuckled. "Okay. Okay. Let me throw some clothes on. I'll be right out."

He shut the door, and I sat down in his gray wooden rocking chair. My eyes danced across the land that Uncle Colt owned. I could understand why everyone who came to the ranch stayed and never left. *Maybe I'll talk to Cowboy again about the idea of movin' into the cabin next door.* Mom and Dad still hadn't made a decision, but they hadn't said no, so there was still hope. I knew I didn't legally need their permission, but I respected them too much to not get their approval. And Uncle Colt required it. I rolled my eyes.

The door squeaked just before Wyatt's boots hit the wood of the porch. "Ready to go?"

"Yes!" I beamed up at him.

"Have you decided what kind of tree and where you want to plant it?"

"Hopefully, somethin' with pink blossoms. And I want to plant it somewhere that Emelia can see it every day."

"Good idea."

I couldn't wait to spend time with Wyatt. He was one of those people who made me feel happy and good whenever he was around.

"How's the wild horse?" I asked as the truck jostled down the road.

"He's perfect. Colt and I are gonna release him tomorrow. Well, we are taking him back to Corolla anyway."

"That's exciting."

"Yeah," Wyatt said, his voice dropping to almost a whisper.

"Aww. What's wrong? You're not happy about him bein' better?"

"No, I'm glad and thankful he's better, but I'm sad to see him go."

"I know you bonded, and I know how attached you get to animals, but it's what's best for him. To go back home. Where he belongs." *Change the subject, Caitlyn. Think. Think.* I didn't want him to be sad while we were out. "How's Minnie?"

"She's good. I think she gets a little sad when I take Flash for a ride and she doesn't get to go."

"Aww. Maybe when I move to the ranch, she'll feel better because I can take her for rides, too."

His brow arched as he glanced over at me. "Your parents gave you their blessin'? I wasn't sure if you were still thinkin' 'bout movin'."

"No." My chin fell to my chest. "They are still thinkin' about it. What do you think about it?"

"I think it'd be great." He coughed. "I mean, that'd be cool."

My heart sank. "So, you don't care one way or the other?"

"I mean, who wouldn't love havin' their best friend livin' next door?"

"Yeah?" My spirits started to rise.

"Of course. I miss hangin' out like we used to."

Heat rose to my cheeks. "Me, too." I flipped the corners of the pages of the sheets in my lap. *I almost forgot.* "Oh, and we need to pass these around."

Wyatt peered over at the flyers in my hand.

"I made flyers for people to come and make pinwheels. Mom and Dad said we could use the café."

"Perfect. We can do that after we get the tree." Wyatt pulled into the parking lot of Earthy Expressions. "Well, here we are."

"Great. Let's see what Mr. Grant can help us come up with."

We passed through the flower shop part of the business, as the trees were in the back.

"Well, hey, you two," Mr. Grant greeted us as we stepped into the area where the trees were located.

"Hey, Mr. Grant," I replied.

"What can I do for ya, Caitlyn?" he asked as he removed his brown work gloves from his hands.

Mr. Grant was an older man. Old enough to be my grandpa. He had grown a belly over the years, but the one thing that remained the same was his mustache. It was a mixture of gray and black to match the hair that peeked out from under his baseball cap. He had started Earthy Expressions before I was even a twinkle in my parents' eyes. Or so the story always went.

"Well, I'm lookin' for a tree that's good to plant in December. Preferably one with pink blooms?" I bit my bottom lip. "It's a gift for Emelia, in honor of Quinn."

"Ah. That's a sweet gift. Quinn was such a delight whenever I saw her. So sad what happened." Mr. Grant cleared his throat. "Well, I think an Eastern Redbud is just the ticket, and just so happens I have one left."

"Yay!" I clapped my hands.

He shifted toward some trees behind him before turning his head to say, "But sad to say, it won't bloom until at least its third year." Mr. Grant set a small tree in front of me. It reminded me of Charlie Brown's Christmas tree. "And it has heart-shaped blossoms, so it's kinda perfect for the occasion. Now, Caitlyn, listen closely. You'll want to soak the root ball for twenty minutes before you plant it. Once you put the ball in the hole, gently break up the root ball so the roots can grow into the soil. And make sure when you dig the hole, it's slightly bigger than the root ball." He wiped his hands on his pants. "Oh, and you'll need some of this." Mr. Grant handed me a small bag.

"And what's this?" I asked, taking the bag from his grasp.

He smiled and tapped the bag with his fingertip. "This here is slow-release fertilizer. It will help the tree grow." His smile was contagious.

"Thank you, Mr. Grant."

"Are ya ready to check out, then?"

"Yes, I think we have all we need."

After paying for the tree and loading it into the back of Wyatt's truck, we jumped in to pass out flyers. "I should give one to Mr. Grant," I realized. "Wait for me." I ran back inside. "Hey, Christy. I forgot to give one of these to Mr. Grant."

"What is it?" She took the flyer from my hand.

"We are making pinwheels in honor of Quinn. Please tell

as many people as you can. Except for Emelia." I smiled and lifted my index finger and pressed it to my lips.

"I'll hang it on the bulletin board, right here." She pushed a tack into the paper.

"Thank you!" I knew Emelia wouldn't see it there. Or anywhere, really. She rarely went out anymore.

I slid back into the truck. Earthy Expressions was just outside of town. On the drive, we rode in silence. As always, it wasn't an awkward silence. Like so many things with Wyatt, it was comfortable. We just enjoyed being together. We handed out flyers to every business and person we saw until we ran out of places to go and flyers to pass out.

"Thanks for helping me today."

"No problem. Anythin' for you, Chipmunk."

When we arrived back at the ranch, my legs bounced up and down. As the engine stopped, I jumped from the truck and made a beeline for the main house. "Uncle Colt! Uncle Colt!" I hollered as soon as my feet were planted on the kitchen floor.

Aunt Callie hustled in from the living room. Her brows furrowed in worry. "What's wrong?"

"Where's Uncle Colt? We got the tree. It's perfect, and we need to plant it!" I shouted without taking a breath.

Aunt Callie laughed. "Slow down. Colt is in the stable, fixing a broken stall door. While you're here, I wanted to let you know I bought all the supplies for the pinwheels."

"You did?" Tears stung my eyes. "Aunt Callie, you didn't have to do that." I wound my arms around her. "Thank you so much."

She enveloped me in her arms. "Of course. I wanted to help. It's such a wonderfully sweet thing you are doing."

"I'm gonna go find Uncle Colt." I gestured with my thumb over my shoulder.

"Okay. Let me know if there's anything else I can do."

I laughed. "You know I will."

I jogged over to the stable. Uncle Colt's and Wyatt's voices were hushed but still drifted over to me just outside the door.

"Just tell her already," Uncle Colt urged Wyatt.

"I will . . . eventually."

My heart stopped in my chest. I had no idea who they were talking about, but an ache formed in my chest as I thought about Wyatt with another woman. I sucked in a deep breath before stepping just inside the door. "Hey, guys."

Both of them startled and looked at me like deer in headlights.

"Oh, hey, Caitlyn. Nice choice on the tree. It's perfect." Uncle Colt nodded toward the tree that was already soaking in water.

A proud smile grew on my lips. "Thanks."

"Have ya decided where ya wanna plant it?"

"Yes. I was thinkin' outside Emelia's cabin. So, whenever she looks out her window, she can see it."

"That's an excellent idea."

Wyatt grabbed a shovel from its hook on the wall as Uncle Colt picked up the tree. "Let's go dig a hole," Wyatt said as he rested the shovel on his shoulder.

I followed them up to the cabins. "What if she sees us?" I hadn't thought about that until that moment.

"Oh, she and Luke just left for a ride so I could fix the door on Tinkerbell's stall," Uncle Colt informed me.

I placed my hand on my heart and let out a breath. "Thank goodness." I pointed to an area a few feet away from Emelia's cabin. "This is the spot I had in mind. What do ya think?"

"I think it's a great spot. She'll be able to see it every mornin' when she's in her kitchen. And when it becomes a mature tree, it won't be too close to the cabins."

Wyatt lifted the shovel from his shoulder and then shoved the end of it into the ground, pulling up a big piece of dirt and grass. It brought with it an earthy, moist, slightly sweet scent.

After the hole was dug, Uncle Colt removed the tree from the bucket of water. "Do you want to do the honors, Caitlyn?"

"I'd love to."

He held it out to me, and I gently took it from his hands. I set it in the hole and broke up the root ball, just like Mr. Grant had instructed, and poured some fertilizer into the hole. I spread the fertilizer around before holding the trunk of the tree as Wyatt shoveled the dirt back around it.

We all stood admiring the tiny tree. It was just like Quinn in a way. It was small but mighty. Except the tree would have the chance to grow and mature. A tear threatened my eye.

My voice lowered. "It's perfect. I can't wait to see it when it blooms."

"Ya did good, kid." Uncle Colt wrapped his arm around my shoulder.

My cheeks grew warm. "Thank you. Uncle Colt, would it be okay if I went and said hello to Minnie and maybe take her for a ride?"

"Well, I don't see why not. Let's go get her tacked up."

"Chip— Caitlyn, could Flash and I go with ya?" Wyatt sucked in a breath. "Unless ya'd rather be alone."

A smile formed on my lips. "I can't speak for Minnie, of course, but I'd love it if ya joined us."

"Great."

"Minnie could use a good run. Callie took her out last week but hasn't had a chance this week."

"Good. Then it'll be a help to everyone." I flashed a satisfied smile.

"Definitely will."

After we saddled up Minnie and Flash, we trotted away from the stable. Wyatt turned his head and hollered back to me, "Let's go to a place you've never been on the ranch . . . well, at least not with me."

"Okay." I squeezed Minnie's sides, attempting to catch up to them. When we were side by side, I asked, "Where do ya wanna go?"

"There's a pretty place at the edge of the property by the river."

"Really? I've never been out that far before."

"Good." A confident smile crossed Wyatt's lips.

As we rode closer to the river, the rapids roared as the water flowed downstream to join the Albemarle Sound. The muted colors of the trees and foliage surrounding the river left no cover for the birds that lived there in the winter months.

I loved living so close to the water. It mellowed out the weather. It was never too hot or too cold in Edenton, at least not to me. Fall and winter were my favorite times of the year, though. Both created air that was crisp and clean and left you breathing in the hope of what was to come.

We stopped just short of the bank. I closed my eyes and deeply inhaled, basking in the peaceful serenity. "I love it here," I confessed as my eyes fluttered open.

"Thought you'd never been here before." Wyatt raised a brow at me.

"I mean Edenton."

"Then why'd ya leave?" he asked solemnly.

"Because I thought I wanted somethin' different." My eyes stayed focused on the water. It was crashing against the shore like my heart was crashing against my ribcage. "But once I was away, I realized what I had and what I wanted. It was here all along."

"And what is it that ya want?"

My breath hitched in my throat at his question. "Well . . . um . . ." *You.* Why couldn't I just say that one simple word out loud?

Because I knew if I said the word out loud, it would be out there. And it left me open for the possibility of so much heartache. Mom and I had talked about my feelings for Wyatt many times. She told me I needed to tell him how I felt. That, yes, I could possibly lose his friendship, but what if he felt the same way? *What if he loves me, too? As more than a friend. No. No. I can't tell him. He deserves so much better than me.*

"You don't have to say if ya don't wanna."

I opened my mouth to say something, but my voice froze in my throat. A sigh escaped my lips as the sun began to set behind the naked trees.

"We'd better get back before it gets dark. It'll be impossible for us to see, and I didn't bring my light with me," Wyatt said, breaking the awkward silence I had created.

"Okay," I whispered, still trying to find my voice.

We turned the horses around and galloped back to the stable. I tried not to think about what I really wanted. I couldn't risk the friendship we had. More so, the fact he'd be saddled with my disease. So, maybe it was for the best that I wasn't able to tell him how I felt.

When we arrived back at the stable, it felt like a lifetime before Wyatt uttered a word. "Let's let them cool down a bit in the corral," he finally said, flopping his saddle across the sawhorse before taking Minnie's from my arms.

"Alright." I grabbed the reins on Minnie and led her to the corral.

Wyatt soon followed with Flash. "I'll get them put up for the night later if ya need to get goin'."

I glanced at my watch. "Yeah, I probably should. Need to take my insulin and eat my carbs for the night." *Another reminder we are better off as friends. For now, anyway.* "Good night, Cowboy." I leaned up and pressed my lips to his cheek. An electric spark shocked my lips. "Thanks for the help with the tree, the ride, and the company."

"Sure. Night, Chipmunk."

Chapter 13

Wyatt

I wasn't ready to say goodbye to the wild horse. But he was healed and needed to get back with his family. "Come on, boy. Don't ya wanna be with your family?" I asked as Colt stood inside the trailer, trying to coax him inside with an apple. Colt tried to pull him in with the lead, but the horse reared up and almost hit his head on the roof of the trailer. "It's okay, buddy," I reassured the horse with the most soothing tone I could muster. "Nothin's gonna hurt ya in there."

"We may have to get Doc Norris out here to help with a sedative or somethin'." Colt hopped down from the trailer. "I don't want him to hurt himself, and he's obviously terrified of the trailer."

I scratched the back of my head. I was out of ideas myself.

Colt plucked his phone from his pocket and hit a series of numbers I could only guess were for the vet. "Hey, Doc, it's Colt." He paused. "Yeah. It's time, but we can't get him in the trailer. Anythin' you can do?" Colt listened. "Okay. Thanks." He lowered his phone. "Doc's on his way."

After some time of Colt and I staring off into space, a truck pulled up to the trailer. "Hey, Doc," Colt greeted Doc Norris after the vet pulled his bag from the truck.

"Hey, Colt. Hey there, Wyatt."

I nodded toward Doc.

"Let's see what we can do for this boy." He gently set his bag on the ground beside the horse. His hands disappeared inside the bag, and when they appeared again, he had a syringe and a small bottle. After removing the needle from the horse, Doc said, "It'll take a few minutes to take effect."

Doc was right. After a few minutes, the horse became wobbly. "Let's try this again," Colt said. He grabbed the lead rope, and sure enough, the horse slowly followed him inside. I latched the door shut, and Colt came around from the door at the front of the trailer. "Well, we'd best get goin'. Thanks, Doc." Colt extended his hand. "Have a good day."

Doc grabbed hold of his hand and shook it. "No problem. Be careful when you get him out. He might be a bit feisty. Travel safe."

"Will do." Colt made his way to the driver's side door and hopped in.

I did the same on the other side. It was a two-hour drive to Corolla in the Outer Banks. "I really hope this goes well," I confessed to Colt.

He blew out a breath. "Me, too, Wyatt. Me, too."

Halfway through the drive, the truck jerked to the left. Colt cut the wheel to the right to straighten up. "Whoa!" Colt checked the rearview mirror. "Hold on, boy. You'll be home and out of the trailer soon."

"Hopefully, that won't happen again." I attempted to slow my heart.

When we finally arrived at Corolla, we drove straight to the office of the Corolla Wild Horse Fund to meet Dustin. They were the people who cared for the wild horses. I checked on the horse while Colt went inside.

"It's okay. You're almost home," I whispered next to the

trailer, where I could see the horse's head almost pressed against the wall.

"So, you can follow me," Dustin told Colt as they walked up to the truck.

"Let's go," Colt called out over the cab of the truck.

We followed behind Dustin to the area where the wild horses resided. I was mesmerized as the herd came into view. *Wow.*

Colt gasped. "Wow! They're gorgeous. I've never seen so many wild horses."

"Me neither."

Dustin stopped in front of us and slid out from his driver's seat. "Ya ready?" he asked as Colt opened his door.

"Yep."

At the back of the trailer, Colt slowly lifted the latch and opened the door. I entered the trailer from the front to coax the horse out. "Come on, buddy. Time to see your family." I grabbed the lead rope and gently pushed him back to get him going. He startled and then slowly began backing out. Once his hooves were on solid ground, he whinnied.

"Okay. Let's check him out." Dustin ran his hand down the horse's flank. "Well, he looks great, especially for the injuries he sustained." Dustin turned his attention to Colt. "Thank you so much for taking such good care of him. And for returnin' him."

"Of course. It was a group effort, and we all know he isn't ours to keep. He'll be missed, though." Colt's eyes flashed in my direction.

As Dustin stepped up to the horse's head, he asked, "Are ya ready to go back to your family now?"

The horse raised and lowered his head. Dustin led him closer to the herd as they stood on the sandy tan beach. The water ebbed and flowed on the shore. It truly was a sight to behold.

Dustin lifted the rope and pulled it over the horse's head. Neither of them moved. The horse's ears moved back and forth as if waiting for an invitation. A mare lifted her head in his direction. She moved her head as if to say, "Come on."

"I wonder if that's his mom," I whispered to Colt.

"I dunno."

That seemed to be all the horse needed, as he took off like a shot over to the other horses.

"Well, it looks like the herd is accepting him back, which is a relief," Dustin noted. "We'll have to make sure to keep an eye on him, just in case they end up rejecting him," he said as he strode over to us, slapping the wound-up rope against his leg.

"That's good to hear." Colt sighed in relief.

"Yeah. I was a little concerned since he's been so close to humans for the amount of time he has been." Dustin held out the lead to Colt.

Colt wrapped his hand around the rope as Dustin released his own. Then, Colt turned to me. "Ready to head back?"

"Let's go home," I said sadly. It was no secret I'd gotten attached to the horse. I climbed into the passenger seat and blew out a long breath.

Chapter 14

Cailtyn

It was three days before Christmas. The day of making pinwheels for Quinn. I wasn't even sure anyone would show up. Callie and I set up tables with pink plastic tablecloths so that after everyone was done, we could throw everything away without a huge hassle.

Mom and Dad had agreed to shut down the café from one o'clock to four o'clock except for pickup orders. I loved the way they loved me and supported me no matter what choices I made. If I fell, they always helped me up. And if I succeeded, they were always there, cheering me on.

When the bells chimed and Wyatt appeared in the doorway, my heart ached. I wished he had grown up knowing love like my parents gave me. I wanted to give him that kind of love for the rest of our time on earth. I sighed. *I'm goin' to do it. I'm goin' to tell him right now.* I marched over to the door.

Wyatt's smile made me weak in the knees. "Hey, Chipmunk," he said softly.

I opened my mouth to tell him exactly how I felt, but the words stuck in my throat, strangling my voice. I swallowed hard. All I could manage to squeak out was, "I'm so glad you're here." A sheepish grin spread across my face.

"What do ya want me to do? Where do ya want me?"

Right beside me until the end of time. Why can't I just say that? UGH! "I think we have everythin' all set up. We are just waitin' on people to come. We had one o'clock on the flyers, so I don't expect anyone to come much before one-thirty."

"Okay. So, we wait." He sat down on a wooden chair.

"I suppose we could make our own pinwheels while we wait," I told him, holding up the paper and rod for the stem.

"Sure. That way we can show them what it's supposed to look like." His face brightened.

Wyatt picked up all the supplies he needed and sat down at one of the tables. I watched as he scribbled something onto the paper before folding it into the pinwheel shape and pushing the pin into the middle. He attached the pinwheel to the stick and put it up to his lips. His mouth formed an "o," and the pinwheel began to spin around. A proud smile formed on his lips. "I did it."

I giggled. "Yes, you did."

Even though Wyatt was a grown man, the childlike wonder inside him was something I adored.

Little girl laughter filled the air before the bells announced their arrival. "Caitlyn!" Lainey shouted as soon as she was inside the café. The rest of the girls—Emma, Grace, and Lilly—joined her in a group hug.

"When are you comin' back to teach us?"

"Oh, I'm not sure, Emma. I haven't talked with Sandee yet." I patted Lilly on the back. "Are ya ready to make some pinwheels for Quinn?"

"Yeah!" they all yelled with their fists in the air.

I escorted them over to the table and showed them all the supplies they would need to make one. Smiling, I watched as they wrote little notes on them. Wyatt, Callie, and I assisted them in pushing the pins into the centers and attaching them to the rods.

"That was fun. I miss Quinn, though." Emma set her pinwheel in the basket and hung her head.

"We all do, sweetie. That's why we are makin' the pinwheels. So we can all remember her for a long, long time."

Emma wrapped her arms around me.

"Mine doesn't look right." Lainey frowned, holding up her pinwheel.

"Oh, that's easy to fix," I told her, placing her pinwheel on the table. "You just didn't get all of the wheel into the pin, that's all." I removed the pin from the center. "Here, you hold down all the flaps, and I'll stick the pin in, okay?"

"Okay." She smiled. With her tongue protruding from her lips, she bent the flaps down so the points were all in the center. "Like this?"

"Yes. Now, hold them in place, and I'll push the pin through." I pushed it through, making sure each flap was underneath before bending the legs of the pin to the back of the pinwheel. "There ya go."

"Thanks, Caitlyn!" Lainey exclaimed before jumping from her seat and running over to the basket and dropping the pinwheel inside.

"Thank you for invitin' us, Caitlyn," Grace said before running out the door.

The other little girls soon followed.

People filed in and out of the café until four o'clock. It warmed my heart to see so many people who wanted to remember Quinn. There would be so many pinwheels to give to Emelia.

Chapter 15

Caitlyn

"**A**re we ready to go see Christmas lights?" I asked everyone as I walked into the living room in my winter pajamas that said "Sister Bear" on them. They were red and black plaid pants. The shirt was gray with plaid sleeves, and the words were plaid, too, matching the pants.

My family sat on the couch in their matching pajamas. Of course, Dad's said "Papa Bear," Mom's read "Mama Bear," and Dyl's "Brother Bear." Mom had found them a couple of years before, and we decided to make it a tradition to wear them when we went to look at Christmas lights on Christmas Eve.

"Let's go," Dad said. "We're supposed to meet the group at the church parking lot before we head out."

Typically, the whole Redemption Ranch family went with us. We would pile into as few cars as possible. I always wished we could have a car big enough to have all of us inside so we could experience the lights together. We started at one end of town and ended at Redemption Ranch.

Uncle Colt went all out at Christmas, decorating the whole ranch. It was a sight to see for sure. He created a walk-through experience that people from all over came for. It was one of the few fundraisers Uncle Colt had each year for the horses.

Everyone was waiting for us when we pulled into the church parking lot. "Hey, everyone!" I waved as I got out of the car.

Wyatt was there, leaning against his truck with his legs crossed. He was looking at his phone. Seeing him every year in his red and black plaid pajamas Mom had given him for Christmas when she bought ours made my heart flutter at a bumble bee's pace. She had them specially made to say "Friend Bear." I wished they said "Boyfriend Bear," but the words would never flow from my mouth.

"Hey, Chipmunk," Wyatt whispered as I approached him.

I smiled. "Hey, Cowboy. How are ya?"

"Better now." His lopsided grin appeared on his face. "Can I ride with ya?"

"Don't ya every year?"

"Well, yeah, but I didn't want to assume."

"It wouldn't be Christmas Eve tradition if ya didn't."

We all piled into two SUVs and set off to look at the lights.

The lights were a little disappointing. There weren't as many as there normally were. It had been that way for the last few years. Maybe because we went earlier in the evening ever since Uncle Colt started the walk-through light exhibit. But I still enjoyed the time with my family, and with Wyatt . . . especially with Wyatt.

Once we were at the ranch, though, my excitement returned. The lights could be seen from the main house. Cars were beginning to line up, waiting for the exhibit to open. Wyatt and I volunteered to help guide cars into temporary parking spots on the backside of the cabins. The entrance to the exhibit started at Quinn's tree. But only Wyatt, Uncle Colt, Aunt Callie, and I knew it was Quinn's tree.

I smiled thinking about Quinn. She would have adored the

lights. I could picture her running through the walkways and yelling for us to look at all the lights, her pigtails bouncing as she went, no doubt in her pink cowgirl boots that Luke had bought for her. She rarely took them off.

After the line of cars dwindled, Wyatt asked, "Ya wanna go look at the lights now?"

"Of course I do."

We made our way over to the entrance. The twinkle lights on the pathway were so bright. Every few feet, on both sides, a couple of large figurines lit up. There was Gingerbread Man, Frosty the Snowman, a John Deere tractor, and some horses. At the end of the last pathway, Santa sat in the sleigh guided by his reindeer. Little elves put presents into the back of the sleigh. Rudolph's nose blinked, and the reins had twinkle lights that sparkled in the night. There was a space in the sleigh for people to get their picture taken with Santa. Christmas carols played, and a hot chocolate bar was set up.

"Want some hot chocolate?" I asked.

"Sure. But before we do, there's somethin' I've been tryin' to tell ya." Wyatt grabbed my hand and twirled me around to face him.

"Yeah? What is it?" *What does he want to say? Has he met someone?* My heart sank to the pit of my stomach as I remembered the conversation I overheard between Uncle Colt and him.

"I've been wantin' to tell ya this for a while now, but I just haven't known how . . ."

"There you both are!" Dad hollered over to us.

Not now, Dad!

"Colt is startin' a bonfire. Let's go."

Wyatt sighed deeply.

"Okay. Be there in a minute," I reluctantly agreed.

"Don't take too long." Dad waved as he turned back in the direction from which he came.

I turned back to Wyatt. "You were sayin'?"

"It can wait. Let's go have some s'mores."

"Are ya sure?" I blew all of the air out of my lungs. I didn't want to hear if he was seeing someone, but I wanted to know what he wanted to say.

"Yeah. Let's go."

* * *

"**G**ood mornin'!" I smiled at Dad in the kitchen. "Merry Christmas!"

Dad kissed the top of my head. "Merry Christmas."

"Mom already at the café?"

"You know it. I'm headin' there myself. Are you comin'?" Dad asked as if it wasn't a tradition to go to the café on Christmas.

"Dad!" I rolled my eyes and giggled.

He laughed as he grabbed his keys from the counter. "I'll see ya later, then. Love you."

"Love you, too."

After Dad closed the door, I ran upstairs to take my morning insulin and get dressed. Not only was it tradition to go to the café for Christmas dinner, it was also tradition to go see Wyatt first thing to exchange gifts.

Mom and Dad always went to the café in the morning to set up and to finish cooking the last of the feast. We usually ate dinner at around three o'clock. I pulled on my jeans and ugly Christmas sweater—also tradition—and jogged down the stairs.

Grabbing my purse and keys, I opened the door and ran out to my car. *I wonder what Cowboy got me this year.* He hadn't asked me what I wanted, like he had every other year. *I'm sure he found the perfect gift.* He always did. He was the best at gift-giving.

I smiled as I turned down the dirt road toward the cabins. Butterflies danced in my stomach. *I hope Cowboy likes what I got him.* I pulled up next to his truck outside his cabin and pushed the button to pop my trunk. As I rounded my car to the trunk, Wyatt's door opened.

"Hey, Chipmunk! Merry Christmas!"

"Hey, Cow— ack!" When I attempted to lift the lid of the trunk, it didn't move, and I lost my balance.

Before I hit the ground, Wyatt's arms were wrapped around me. "Careful." His breath brushed my ear, and goosebumps spread like wildfire down my arms. He chuckled as he helped me back to standing firmly on the ground. "Trunk stuck again?"

"Thanks, and apparently." Heat radiated up my neck and over my cheeks.

Wyatt stuck his fingers under the lid, where the release lever was. He jiggled the lid, and it finally popped open.

"Ah, my hero," I swooned.

"Let's get inside. It's a little chilly out this mornin'." Wyatt ran his hands up his arms.

"Well, what are ya doin' out here in just a T-shirt and pajama pants, silly?" I plucked the box from the depths of my trunk.

Wyatt's eyes lit up. "Obviously rescuing a damsel in distress. Is that for me?" He pointed at the box.

"Yeah. Unless ya want it to be for someone else. I'm sure Uncle Colt would love it." I giggled as I turned to drop the box back into my trunk.

Wyatt's hands flew to the box, snatching it from my grasp.

"No. No. There's no need for that." He turned on his heel and fled to his cabin.

I shook my head and softly laughed. Oh, that man had every bit of my heart. *God give me the right words at the right time.*

All in My time, My child.

I stepped inside the cabin. The only lights on were the Christmas tree in the far corner of the living room and around the top of the shelf by the door. "Oh, Cowboy. It looks like a Hallmark Christmas movie in here."

He chuckled. "Thanks. I think. Can I open this now?" He held the box up next to his ear and shook it before plopping down on his couch.

"Of course." I slowly lowered myself next to him. I held my breath, hoping he would like it. *I should have gotten him something else.*

Wyatt carefully removed the paper.

"Cowboy, just rip into it."

"But the paper's so nice."

"Just do it." I laughed.

He finally ripped the paper before removing the lid and tossing the tissue paper into the air. He let out a small gasp.

Oh no! He hates it!

"Chipmunk." He lifted the hat from the box. "You didn't have to do that." He inspected it from every angle.

"Do you like it? You mentioned one time that you wanted a nice hat to wear when you go out. If you don't like it, we can return it." I reached out to grab the hat.

He lifted it in the air out of reach. "I don't like it." He paused, causing my heart to sink into my stomach. "I *love* it!" His smile spread from ear to ear as he slid the hat onto his head.

"You *do*?" My hope returned. "Did I get the right size?"

"Fits like a glove. Thank you so much!"

"Merry Christmas, Cowboy."

"I guess it's your turn now, huh?" He stood from his place on the couch and disappeared down the hall.

"You didn't have to get me anythin'." I said that every year, but secretly, I was so happy he didn't listen.

He tilted his head down and stared at me when he returned to the room. "You know we do this every year, Chipmunk. I know I don't *have* to get ya anythin'. Just like ya don't have to get *me* anythin'. But we do it anyway because we're best friends."

How did he always manage to make me blush? "I know."

He stood in front of me, holding out in the palm of his hand a small square package that was beautifully wrapped in shiny silver paper with white snowflakes on it and a red ribbon.

I gently lifted the present from his palm. "It's so pretty. I almost don't want to open it . . . almost."

"Yeah. The store put it in a bag. It was nice, but I didn't feel like it was special enough. Emelia helped me wrap it." He sat down beside me. "Open it."

I carefully untied the bow.

"Chipmunk, just rip into it," he said, mocking me.

But I didn't listen. I slid my finger between the paper and the tape, trying my hardest not to rip the paper. As I slipped the paper from the navy-blue box and saw the name of the jeweler stenciled in gold, my eyes shot to his face. "What did you do?" I pulled the top from the bottom of the box. *It's too big of a box for a ring. What are you talkin' about, Caitlyn? You aren't even dating.* With my heart pounding, I peered inside and gasped. "Cowboy, this is too much. It's gorgeous, but I can't accept it." I held the box out to him.

"Of course you can. It was meant for you." He smiled that smile that made my heart melt. Every. Single. Time. He pressed his hands to the top of mine and guided the box back to me.

My eyes were drawn back to the box as the pink and white stones sparkled in the lights of the Christmas tree. "Will you put it on me?" I held the box back out to him as a tear threatened my inner eye.

"Yeah." His hands shook as he lifted the necklace from the cream-colored pad that was holding it in place.

I lifted my hair away from my neck and turned away from him. His hands appeared on each side of my face before he separated the ends of the chain and drew it to my neck.

"Ya know why I picked a snowflake?" His voice was low and raspy. His breath tickled my neck, sending electricity down my body.

"No. Why?" My voice cracked.

"Because each snowflake is unique. As they float to the ground, each one takes a different path, but they always land right where they're supposed to land. Each one a piece of perfection from heaven. Just like you." He pressed his lips to the top of my head. "There ya go."

I turned and faced him as the tear that had threatened to fall fell to my cheek. "Cowboy, that may be the best thing anyone has ever said to me." I stood on my tiptoes and grazed his cheek with my lips. "Thank you so much. I love it." I shuffled to the mirror in the hallway to admire it.

"Ya really like it?" Hope filled his voice.

"Yes. I absolutely do. It's by far the most beautiful gift anyone has ever given me." I wrapped my arms around his middle.

Wyatt sighed, and his body relaxed.

"Shall we get to the café to help set up?" I suggested.

"After we say hi to Uncle Colt and Aunt Callie, of course. Even though they will be there later, too."

"Let's go." Wyatt settled his new hat on his head.

"You don't want to get dressed first?" I laughed.

He looked down. "Oh. That would probably be a good idea." He removed his hat and held it out to me before rushing off to his room and closing the door. A few minutes passed before he emerged from his room. He stole his hat from my hands and plopped it back on his head. "How about now? Ready to go?"

I studied him in his "ugly" Christmas sweater, with a Christmas tree on it that actually lit up, and his Wranglers. "You don't want to wait for a special occasion to wear that?"

"Chipmunk, with you, every day is a special occasion." He winked and grinned. "Do ya wanna ride together or separate?"

His comment, or compliment rather, caught me off guard. I tripped over the threshold and ran smack dab into Wyatt's chest as he turned to shut the door behind me. "Oof."

"Careful." He reached out to steady me as his breath caressed the top of my head. I had no idea the mere touch of Wyatt's breath on my hair would cause so much heat to course through my veins. "You okay now?" he asked, lowering his hands.

"Ye . . . yeah." My voice shook. *What is happening between us?* I felt a shift but wasn't one hundred percent positive it wasn't a figment of my imagination. *Does he feel the same way about me that I do about him?* Once I'd regained my composure, I was finally able to respond to his question. "I'd like to ride together, if that's okay."

"Anythin' ya want." He smiled.

We stopped at the main house before heading to the café. Wyatt parked his truck outside the massive white house. I ran up the stairs, not waiting for him, and I plowed into the kitchen.

"Merry Christmas!" I shouted.

Aunt Callie and Uncle Colt came into the room at the same time from opposite sides of the kitchen. "Hey, Caitlyn! Merry Christmas!" Aunt Callie's smile spread from ear to ear as she enveloped me in a hug.

I deeply inhaled. Aunt Callie wasn't my parent, but she was family. She felt like home just as much as my blood family.

"Hey, kiddo. Hey, Wyatt. Merry Christmas! What are you two up to?" Uncle Colt pulled me into a hug as I was leaving Callie's arms.

"We exchanged presents like we do every year. And just wanted to stop by before heading to the café. You both are comin', right?"

"Of course. It's tradition, isn't it?" Uncle Colt asked.

As a tear formed in the corner of my eye, my voice cracked. "What about Emelia and Luke? I haven't seen them much since I've been home."

"They've been keepin' to themselves a lot. They're grievin', and we've been givin' them the space to do that. So, I'm not sure if they'll come or not, but they know they're both invited," Uncle Colt attempted to reassure me. He ran his hand across my shoulder.

"Okay." I couldn't hide my disappointment.

"So, what did ya get each other?" Uncle Colt said, quickly changing the subject. Glancing at Wyatt and pointing to his head, he said, "I'm assumin' the hat."

Wyatt smiled and nodded.

"Looks great. Nice choice, Caitlyn."

Wyatt's chest puffed out. "It's my goin' out hat."

"It's perfect," Aunt Callie chimed in. "What did you get, Caitlyn?"

I had my fingers wrapped around the pendant hanging from my neck. I let it fall to my chest.

Aunt Callie gasped. "Wyatt. It's gorgeous." She lifted the snowflake and held it in her fingertips.

"Good job, Wyatt." Uncle Colt patted Wyatt's shoulder.

Wyatt's smile grew wider as his shoulders fell back, and his chest puffed out again.

My heart fluttered. *Oh, this man.* "We'd better get goin'. Mom and Dad will need our help settin' up."

"We'll see ya there a little later," Uncle Colt said as he opened the door for us.

As I climbed into the truck, I asked, "Can we stop by my house? I forgot the present I have for Emelia. In case she and Luke do come."

"Of course."

"Thanks."

We rode in silence on the way to my house. I was too busy working up the courage and confidence to try again to tell him how I felt. I couldn't tell him in the truck, though, because what if he rejected me? I'd be like a trapped rabbit. I'd never survive that.

I wiped my sweaty palms down my thighs as we pulled up to the curb in front of my house. As I unbuckled my seatbelt, I said, "I won't be long."

"Take your time," I heard Wyatt say as I jumped down to the ground before running up to the front door.

Once inside, I barreled up the stairs and into my room. The small red box with a gold bow was right where I'd left it on the corner of my dresser, where I'd thought I wouldn't forget it. But I did. I rolled my eyes and snatched the box from its perch before hurrying back down the stairs and out to where Wyatt was waiting.

When my eyes found him, I stopped dead in my tracks. My heart fluttered rapidly, and my knees went weak. He was leaning against his truck. His legs were crossed at the ankles, and his thumbs were through his belt loops. He wasn't other people's idea of a heartthrob, but he sure made my heart thump. His eyes were focused on the ground with his cowboy hat hiding most of his face, except his mouth.

Oh, how I want to kiss that mouth. He's gonna be the death of me. No time for that, Caitlyn. Gotta get the café to help Mom, Dad, and Dyl. I willed my feet to move forward. "Ya ready?"

"Yep!" Wyatt pushed himself off his truck and opened the passenger door.

Always the gentleman. "Thank you." I climbed up onto the seat.

He tipped his hat and closed the door. Then, he drove the minute down the road to the café. "Can you get the present out of the glovebox for me?" he asked before we got out of the truck.

"Sure. What is it?"

"Somethin' for Emelia," he responded, lifting the box from my hands.

"Oh, that's sweet of you." One of the many things I loved about him. He was always thinking of others.

The bells jingled as we stepped inside.

"Sis! It's about time. I've been slavin' away!" Dyl shouted as soon as the door shut. "Hey, Wyatt!"

"Sorry, Dyl." I laughed. "Where should we start?"

"You can help by finishing up the tables."

"Okay." My eyes searched the room. When my gaze reached Wyatt, I said, "Let's do this."

"Alright."

I found the blue plastic bin that contained the tablecloths and centerpieces. Running my hand over the soft fabric—it felt like flannel—I unfolded the tablecloth. It was red and green plaid with flecks of gold. The flecks reminded me of the gold in Wyatt's eyes, especially in the sunlight. I could get lost in those eyes forever.

"You okay?" he asked from beside me as he pulled at one end of the tablecloth.

Heat rose to my cheeks for what felt like the hundredth time that morning. "Yeah."

He draped his end over the table and smoothed it out. "Why don't I continue with the tablecloths, and you can follow up with the centerpieces?" he suggested.

"That sounds like a good idea." I set the first centerpiece in the middle of the rectangular table. It was a large white candle with small poinsettias around the base with battery-operated white twinkle lights intertwined.

After setting the last centerpiece in place, Wyatt and I stood in the corner, admiring the work.

"It looks great," Wyatt said.

"We always make a great team."

"Yes. Yes, we do. I'm gonna go use the restroom. Be right back."

"Okay."

After he walked away, I slipped out the front door, holding the bells so they didn't announce my departure. I needed some time with God, so I walked the short distance to the lighthouse.

Chapter 16

Wyatt

I stepped out of the restroom and into an empty dining room. Laughter echoed from the kitchen. None of it sounded like Caitlyn's sweet laughs. *Where'd she go?*

I headed outside into the crisp air. The wind wasn't blowing, so it didn't feel as cold as it normally did on Christmas Day. I surveyed the area around the café. She was nowhere in sight. *The water maybe?*

My mind wandered along with my feet. Stuffing my hands into my jacket pockets, I briskly made my way to investigate if my hunch was right.

My thoughts went to the last Christmas I'd had with my parents. It was one of the few times I remembered them being sober. I didn't get much that year, but I had my mom and dad. We sat around the Christmas tree; it was never a large tree, though. Not like the ones I'd seen in Edenton. It wasn't long after that when my parents left me. That Christmas was forever etched into my memory.

Wonder what Chipmunk's doin' out here. I glanced out to the water. It was always so peaceful there. Even if people were around. The beauty of God's work never ceased to amaze me. But Caitlyn was nowhere to be found. *The lighthouse?* I tiptoed up the ramp and onto the landing.

"Lord, give me the courage and the wisdom to say what I need to say," Caitlyn's voice drifted to the end of the light-house.

Wonder what she's talkin' 'bout. What does she want to say? And to whom?

My eyes wandered over to where she was sitting with her legs dangling over the edge of the deck. Her arms were hanging over the bottom railing. She looked so cute kicking her legs back and forth. Like a little kid whose feet didn't reach the floor.

A pang shot through my heart. I pictured Quinn sitting there with Caitlyn, her long blonde hair in braids and asking a million questions. Quinn would've loved this spot. I sighed. It must have been louder than I thought because, at that moment, Caitlyn turned her head in my direction. I swallowed hard.

Caitlyn's eyes grew wide. "How long have you been standin' there?"

Heat shot from my neck, straight to my cheeks. I shoved my hands back into my pockets. *Long enough.* "Not very long. I thought I might find ya here."

"Oh." She patted the space next to her. "Care to join me?"

As I lowered myself to sit, my foot slipped, and my back-side collided with wood. *Smooth, Wyatt. Real smooth.*

"There's actually somethin' I wanted to talk to you about," Caitlyn said as if nothing out of the ordinary had just happened.

I slowly blew out a breath. *Was she talkin' to God about me?* "Okay."

She twisted her hands in her lap. "Well, there's somethin' I've been tryin' to tell ya since I came home . . ."

"Alright. What is it? Ya can tell me anythin'. You know that." *What does she want to tell me? Did she meet someone?* My heart sank at the thought.

"Well . . ." Her phone chimed from the back pocket of her jeans. She pulled it out and opened the message. "Emelia's at the café," she told me, placing her phone back in her pocket. "Let's go."

"Thought ya had somethin' to tell me?"

She latched onto the railing, pulled herself up, and started toward the ramp. I let out an audible breath and followed her. Our conversation would have to wait.

The short distance back to the café seemed like the longest, most silent walk. I didn't want to say anything. I wanted her to tell me what she wanted to say on her own terms, no matter how much the curiosity was killing me.

The bells signaled our entrance into the café, and everyone's attention was on us.

"There she is!" Colt's voice rang out. "Where've ya been? We've been waitin' on ya."

Caitlyn's cheeks turned a pale shade of pink. "Oh, sorry."

Mrs. Logan wrapped an arm around her shoulders. "Well, Dad, Uncle Colt, Aunt Callie, and I wanted to give you your last Christmas present."

"Oh? I didn't know you had anythin' else for me."

"Well, that's because it was a secret," Colt chimed in.

Callie held out a key with the ring pinched between her fingers.

Caitlyn put her palm under the dangling key, and Callie let the key fall. "What's this?"

"It's a key. Duh." Dyl bumped Caitlyn's shoulder.

"Yeah. I see that. But what does it go to?" Her eyes darted among the four adults.

"Well." Mr. Logan stepped forward. "We've decided to say yes to you movin' out to the ranch. It's a probationary period. You have to attend classes and do your chores and keep your diabetes in check. Or you'll have to move back home."

Caitlyn's eyes beamed, and her mouth fell open as she bounced up and down. "Really?"

"Really. Do you agree to the terms?"

"Yes!" She leapt into her dad's arms. "Thank you."

She hugged each of the adults. After hugging Callie, she realized Emelia was standing next to Callie.

"Emelia. I have somethin' for ya."

Emelia's eyes widened. "You do?"

Caitlyn found her jacket in the corner where she'd laid it when we had first arrived. When she was back in front of Emelia, she raised a box toward her,

"Oh, Caitlyn, you didn't have to get me anything." Emelia's eyes became glassy.

Caitlyn smiled. "I know, but when I saw this, I just *had* to get it."

Emelia pulled the top of the box off and dipped her hand inside. Gasps were heard around the room when she pulled out a Precious Moments figurine of a little blonde girl attempting to put a star on top of the Christmas tree. A tear dropped from Emelia's eye as she gently placed the figurine back in the box.

"It reminded me of Quinn." Caitlyn shrugged as her lip quivered. Emelia pulled her into a hug. "I miss her so much," Caitlyn whispered into Emelia's hair.

Emelia left Caitlyn's arms. "I do, too. So so much, especially today. But it makes my heart happy to know she was so loved here." She swiped her cheek with her index finger and held up the box. "This is a beautiful gift. Thank you. I will cherish it forever."

I cleared my throat. "I have a gift for you, too."

"You do? I'm not sure my heart can take much more, but okay." Emelia deeply inhaled.

I held out the box, suddenly second-guessing myself for giving it to her on that day.

"You didn't have to get me anything either, Wyatt." She pulled the box from my grasp.

"I didn't. I made it." I smiled.

"You did?" She removed the lid, moved the tissue paper, and inhaled as she lifted the horse from the box. "Oh, Wyatt. This is absolutely gorgeous."

"Thank you. It's Tinkerbell."

"And Quinn's boots." She ran the tip of her index finger over the little pink boots dangling from the horse's mouth. "I love it, Wyatt. Thank you. I will cherish this forever, also." She grabbed my arm and pulled me into a hug.

"Okay." Mr. Logan clapped his hands together. "Are we all ready to eat?"

"Yes!" Dyl's voice echoed above everyone else's, which caused laughter to ring out.

"Luke, would you like to say grace?"

"Me?" He cleared his throat. "Um. Sure?"

Everyone bowed their heads, joined hands, and closed their eyes.

"Father, God, we thank You for this bountiful feast. We thank You for the friends and family around the room. We ask for Your loving arms to wrap around us and give us extra comfort today . . ." Luke paused and cleared his throat again. "Thank You, Lord, for Your most precious gift of Jesus on this most blessed day. His birthday. May we continue to shine Your light in our actions and our attitudes. We love You, Lord. In the mighty name of Jesus. Amen."

"Amen," echoed around the room.

"Okay, everyone!" Mrs. Logan shouted above the voices. "There's plenty of food to go around. Please enjoy."

People shuffled to the long tables with the turkey and all the fixings spread out over them. I took a second to take in the moment. I found myself doing that a lot in the last few months. We'd lost so much at Redemption Ranch with the death of Quinn, but the whole town had felt the loss, too.

I heard a little girl's giggles. They were soft. Like from a distance. It sounded just like Quinn. I smiled as I felt her presence in the room.

"What're ya grinnin' about?" Cailtyn asked, butting my arm with her shoulder.

"Nothin'. Just feel like Quinn's here." My cheeks flushed at the admission. Not sure why it embarrassed me. Especially because I knew out of everyone in the world, she'd understand.

"Yeah. I feel it, too."

We stood beside each other in silence for a little longer. Sometimes, these were my favorite times with Caitlyn. These little moments frozen in time in the hidden places of my mind.

My eyes scanned the room. Laughter sang through the air like a Christmas carol. Even Emelia laughed. Proof we were alive during this most joyous and festive season.

Thank you, Jesus, for the gift of hearing Quinn's giggles and seeing Emelia smile and laugh. Even if it doesn't last past today.

"Ya ready to eat?" Caitlyn's voice broke me from my prayer.

"I thought ya'd never ask." I smiled down at her.

After filling our plates, we found a couple of empty seats across from Carl and Marie.

"Hey, kids." Marie smiled and waved.

Carl was deep in conversation with Jesse.

"Hi, Marie," Caitlyn responded, setting her plate on the table.

I studied Caitlyn as she counted the carbs on a piece of paper that Mrs. Logan undoubtedly handed her at some point. She took out her insulin pen and turned the dial. "I'll be right back," she told me before escaping to the restroom.

I watched as she returned to the room and flitted around, talking to people like a little butterfly. I knew she wasn't only doing it to be social, though. Caitlyn was doing it to wait out the fifteen minutes before she could eat. I patiently sat and waited for her. Just like I always did when we shared a meal together. And just like always, when she sat back down beside me, she said, "You didn't have to wait for me."

I smiled. "I know."

As we ate, we made small talk with those around us. The turkey disintegrated on my tongue. Delicious. I stabbed another piece of turkey and dipped my fork in the pile of mashed potatoes on my plate.

"Are ya ready to present Quinn's tree to Emelia?" I whispered in Caitlyn's ear.

"Yes. I can't wait." She popped a piece of apple in her mouth. Swallowing, she said, "I also can't wait to move to the ranch. Would ya help me move my stuff after I pack?"

"Of course. Just tell me when."

She danced in her seat. "Thanks."

When our plates were empty, we placed them in the plastic bin.

"Mom, do ya need us to stay and help clean up?" Caitlyn asked.

Mrs. Logan swung her arm around Caitlyn's shoulders. "Don't you have one last gift to give? Why don't you go and do that. If, when you're done, we still have things left to do, you can come back."

"Thanks, Mom."

As Caitlyn was grabbing her jacket from the corner, I asked Mrs. Logan, "Could I take a plate of food for someone?"

"Of course, Wyatt. Help yourself. I'll get you a to-go box."

"Thank you."

When she returned from the kitchen, she carried a white foam container. "Here you go." Her smile always warmed my heart. Maybe it was because her smile looked just like Caitlyn's. I guess that would be the other way around.

I piled food into the container and closed it up. When I spun around, I almost hit Caitlyn with it.

"Who's that for?" Her brows furrowed in confusion.

A sheepish grin spread across my face. "I thought I'd take it to my mom. Do ya mind if we stop by the motel first?"

"Su . . . sure," Caitlyn stuttered as she climbed into my truck.

"Could you hold this for me?"

She took the container from my hands without saying a word.

My heart was about to beat out of my chest. *What am I doin'? Am I really gonna go see her again?* It was the right thing to do.

I pulled into the parking space outside the door to my mom's room. I turned off the engine but stayed glued to my seat.

"Aren't ya gonna go in?" Caitlyn asked.

"Yeah. I just need a second."

We sat there in silence for what seemed like eternity. Then, I sucked in a deep breath, and I smacked my hands on my thighs. "Okay. I'm ready."

"Do you want me to go with ya?"

"No. This is somethin' I've got to do on my own. I won't be long, though." I picked up the container she had set on the center console.

"Okay. Take your time," she softly responded.

I stood in front of my mom's door. Frozen. I finally managed to get my fist up to the door and tap my knuckles against it.

After a few minutes, the door crept open. Mom stood in the doorway with a stunned expression. "Wyatt. I wasn't expectin' to see you here again."

"I know. I just wanted to bring you some Christmas dinner. Hope that's okay." I felt like that little boy again on our last Christmas Day together.

"Do ya wanna come in?"

"No. I have someone waitin' in the car for me."

"Oh." Her shoulders slumped. "Another time, then?"

"Yeah." I scratched the back of my head. "Maybe." I handed her the container of food.

"Thank you for this. Merry Christmas, Wyatt."

"Merry Christmas."

I didn't hear the door close until I had turned on my heels and started to walk away. When I slipped back into the driver's seat, Caitlyn groaned. "What's wrong?" I asked.

"I forgot the pinwheels at my house. Can we go back and get them?"

"Of course." *Any excuse to spend more time with you, Chipmunk.*

Setting my mind on the pinwheels and the tree distracted me from the sight of my mother and her bloodshot eyes. I wasn't sure if she was using again, but she sure looked like it. I hoped I was wrong.

Once we were finally back at the ranch, Caitlyn knocked on Emelia's door. The door slowly widened, and Emelia's bloodshot eyes stared back at us. She swiped her nose with a crumpled tissue. My mother's face flashed through my mind. Could her eyes have been red because she was crying like Emelia was? I hoped it was that instead of my first thought. I chided myself for automatically thinking the worst. *Forgive me, Lord.*

"Hey, Emelia," Caitlyn softly greeted her.

"Hey, Caitlyn. What's up?" She glanced down at the basket in Caitlyn's arms.

"Well, I have another gift for you. If you're up for it. Will you come with us?"

"Um. Okay. Luke?"

"What's goin' on?" Luke asked, appearing behind Emelia and resting his hands on her shoulders.

"Caitlyn said she's got another gift for me. Do you want to come?" She placed her hand on top of Luke's.

"Of course, I want to."

We all strode over to the other side of Emelia's cabin.

"We planted this tree in remembrance of Quinn. It's an Eastern Redbud. It will have pink, heart-shaped blooms."

"You did what?" Emelia's hand flew to her heart. "Oh, Caitlyn, you didn't have to do this."

Caitlyn flashed a bright smile. "I know. But I wanted to. There's somethin' else, too. Everyone made pinwheels with a message to Quinn that I wanted to place around the tree."

"What?" Emelia peeked inside the basket. She reached her hand inside and pulled one out. "There's got to be a hundred in there."

"Quinn left an impression on so many people in the time she was here. I just wanted to show you how loved she was. How loved *you* are."

"Caitlyn." Emelia's lip trembled as she pulled Caitlyn into a hug.

"And we planted it right outside your window." Caitlyn pointed over her shoulder. "So, you'll be the first to see it when it blooms."

"I love that." Emelia smiled.

"Why don't ya read what's on the pinwheel?" Caitlyn nodded at the pink and white pinwheel twirling in the slight breeze.

"Quinn, I miss you. You were a good dance friend. Love, Emma." Emelia ran her fingers over the words on the pinwheel before placing her fingers over her lips. "Could I take these and read them? I don't want them to get ruined by the weather. Maybe I could hang them in my cabin?"

Caitlyn stood there. "Um. Sure. I don't see why not." She held out the basket to Emelia.

Taking it, Emelia said, "Thank you so much for doing this, Caitlyn. It was such a thoughtful gift. The gifts you and Wyatt have given me this Christmas are the most special gifts I've ever been given. Besides Quinn, of course." A tear dripped from her eye and left a lonely trail down her cheek as she moved past us toward her cabin.

"Well, that didn't quite go as I'd planned." Caitlyn's eyes were fixated on her feet.

"I know, but she loved it." I swung my arm over her shoulder and drew her close. "Maybe this summer we could put them around the tree. Ya know, when the weather is better."

"Yeah. I suppose you're right." Her lips formed a half smile, and she held up the key Callie had given her. "Do ya wanna check out my cabin with me?"

"Sure." I didn't want to sound *too* excited, but the truth was, I never wanted to not be around Chipmunk.

Once we were at the door, Caitlyn slid the key into the lock and turned the knob. "I'm so excited," she screeched as she pushed the door open.

I chuckled. "I can't tell at all."

She twirled around the empty living room as I shut the door behind me. "I can't wait to make this place my own." Her smiled shone so brightly.

I couldn't wait for her to be my neighbor, but I definitely couldn't tell her that. "When ya plannin' on movin' in?"

"As soon as possible. Especially because I have to start my EMT classes after the first of the year. I forgot to tell ya that I got my acceptance letter in the mail the day before Christmas Eve. Maybe later this week?" Caitlyn shrugged her shoulders.

"Congratulations. Let me know if and when ya need help."

"I will." She smiled. "Have I told ya lately how blessed I am to have ya in my life?"

Heat crept up my neck. "No. But I don't mind hearin' it. I'm pretty blessed to have you, too."

Just tell her, you idiot. Rip the band-aid off. No! She deserves more than what I have to offer. I don't want to be what holds her back from her dreams. I shook the argument from my head.

"Well, I guess I'd better head back to the café to see if there's anythin' left to do before I go home and start packin'."

My heart deflated. "Yeah. Okay. I've got some chores to do as well."

"I'll text ya later," she said as she locked the door after we stepped onto her porch. "Thank you again for the beautiful necklace."

"You're welcome. Thanks for the hat." I flipped my finger on the brim.

She threw her arms around my neck and nestled into me. Man, how I wished she'd stay there forever. But much too soon, she left my arms.

"Enjoy the rest of your evenin'," Caitlyn said. She slid into her car and drove away.

The last thing I wanted to do on Christmas Day was chores, but they had to be done. I sighed and made my way to the stable.

Chapter 17

Caitlyn

It was New Year's Eve. I had just unpacked the last box of my things and put everything in its place. "There. All done." I wiped my forehead with my arm.

Everyone had pitched in to help me move my stuff to the ranch. Except Luke and Emelia. I was so sad I didn't get to spend more time with them, but I knew they both were still healing. Especially Emelia.

I was excited about the party in the barn later. I had already laid out my outfit on my bed: a black sweater that hit just above my waist and a silver sequin skirt that fell to just above my knees with lace-up black peep-toe heels. Was it really New Year's Eve without sparkles? Definitely not.

My parents had given me some furniture they had stored away. They said it was my birthday present. I had everything I needed for my own little space. *My space.* I loved the sound of that. And the feel. As much as I loved my family, I wanted a place that was all my own. But they weren't too far away when I needed them.

My eyes danced across the room as a smile spread across my lips. All that was left to do was grocery shopping . . . for when I didn't get up in time and missed breakfast at Uncle Colt's. I also couldn't wait to get my hands dirty with chores.

Uncle Colt already assigned Minnie to me as my horse. *My own horse!* I bounced up and down just thinking about it. I pulled my boots onto my feet, grabbed my jacket, and headed to the stable.

For some reason, Wyatt had been scarce since moving my stuff into the cabin. Maybe he wasn't as excited to have me as a neighbor as I'd thought. My heart plummeted to my stomach. *Maybe I'll see him at the stable.*

I had no idea what I'd do once I was at the stable because Uncle Colt hadn't given me any chores yet. He said he'd give me something to do once I'd been there for a week. I was okay with that.

When I stepped into the stable, it was empty except for the horses. "Hi, Warrior. How are ya?" I caressed the side of his head and kissed his nose. "See ya later, buddy." The stall next to him was empty. It was Flash's stall. *Cowboy must have taken him for a ride.*

Minnie stuck her head out of her stall. "Hey, girl. How are ya?" I ran my hand down her nose. "Wanna go for a ride? I only have a couple of hours before the party."

I turned to get the blanket and saddle I'd used before and instantly felt light-headed. As I leaned onto the sawhorse to lower myself to a hay bale, the sawhorse fell over, causing the saddle to hit the floor with a thud. I put my head between my knees. My blood sugar alarm blared from my back pocket. I read the number: 200. *Too high.*

I slowly rose from the hay bale and trudged to the main house. "Aunt Callie!" I stumbled into the kitchen.

Aunt Callie rushed to my side. "What's going on?"

"My blood sugar is too high."

"Your mom gave me an insulin pen before she left the other day, just in case you needed it." She helped me to the closest chair before going to the counter. I heard a drawer open.

Aunt Callie set the pen and an alcohol wipe down in front of me. My shaky hand reached out and took the pen. I wasted no time turning the dial to the correct dosage. I cleaned the site with the wipe, pinched my stomach, and pushed the button, causing the needle to shoot out and into my skin. *Please let it work fast.*

"Are you okay now?" Aunt Callie asked, sitting in the chair next to me.

I lowered my head on the table. I sucked in a deep breath as I felt my body start to move toward normal. "Yeah, I think I will be in a minute." I lifted my head. "Thank you for bein' here."

I swiped my phone from my pocket and checked the number: 197. *It's goin' down.* "Could I get some water?"

"Of course." Aunt Callie rose from her seat and quickly went to the cabinet. I heard ice clink in the glass before the plastic cap being twisted off a water bottle. She slid the glass across the table.

I lifted the glass from the table and drank in the liquid to satisfy my parched mouth. "Thank you. Not a real great start to my time here." I sighed.

Aunt Callie swept her hand across my back. "It's okay. These things happen. Your uncle and I are happy and excited to have you here."

A smile spread across my lips. "Really?"

"Yes. We wouldn't have agreed to it if we weren't." She returned a huge, toothy smile.

Uncle Colt had always been a part of my life. I guess deep down, I hadn't really realized how much until that moment.

I drank some more water and continued to check my sugar level. Slowly, it went back down to some semblance of normal.

I carefully stood from the chair, and once I felt steady, I said, "I'm goin' to go back to the stable. Thank you again."

Aunt Callie rose from her seat. "No problem. Always here for you." She wrapped her arm around my shoulders. "Be careful."

"I will."

I slowly and steadily made my way back to the stable. As I rounded the corner and stepped inside the door, I plowed right into Wyatt, bouncing off his chest like a rubber ball. I closed my eyes, preparing for the hard thud my body was going to make on the ground. But my body didn't hit the dirt, and no pain shot through it, either. I opened one eye to see Wyatt extremely close.

Wyatt's arms were wrapped around my middle. "Sorry, Chipmunk. I didn't see ya there." He set me upright. "You okay?"

I opened my other eye as my heart skipped a beat.

Wyatt studied my face and ran the back of his fingers down my cheek. His brow furrowed with worry. "What's wrong, Chipmunk?"

I let out a breath and leaned into his touch. "I'm okay. My blood sugar got too high, and I got dizzy. I was able to make it to the main house, and Aunt Callie helped me."

"That would explain the saddle and blanket on the ground and the sawhorse overturned."

My eyes widened. "I'm sorry, Cowboy. I'll go clean up my mess."

He grabbed my wrist. "I already took care of it. You look exhausted."

"Yeah. It usually zaps me of energy. I really wanted to ride Minnie before the party."

"Well, you're not doin' that today." Wyatt lifted me into

his arms. "You need to rest, and I'm gonna make sure ya do."

"Cowboy! Put me down. Please." I tried to sound stern, but weariness didn't allow it. I just didn't have the energy to argue. I nestled into his chest and rested my head on his shoulder as I allowed my depleted energy to overtake me.

* * *

I felt someone's hand running down my head. Confusion swirled. *Where am I?* My body still felt heavy as I opened my eyes and surveyed the room. I was lying on my side. On the couch. In my cabin. *That's right. Cowboy carried me back here.* The light of the TV cast a warm glow over the room. The sound was almost mute. It was dark outside my living room window. *Oh no! The party!*

"You didn't wake me up for the party," my raspy voice cried as I lifted my head off Wyatt's leg and peered up at him.

"You needed to rest. Everyone else agreed with me." He removed his hand from my hair and spread his arm over the back of the couch.

I rubbed my eyes with the backs of my hands. "What time is it?"

Wyatt lifted his wrist to check his watch. "It's almost midnight. In about five minutes."

I quickly shot up to my knees. "Can we at least watch the ball drop on TV?"

"Sure." He grabbed the remote from the side table and clicked the button until Times Square appeared on the screen.

I was upset I'd missed the big party in the barn. It was something I looked forward to every year. Almost as if it were an extra birthday party for me. *I'm gonna kiss Cowboy when the ball drops.* I set myself up to do it. I just hoped I didn't chicken out. *No, you won't chicken out. It's time. You'll do it.*

At least if Wyatt rejected me, we'd be the only two in the world who would know about it—and my broken heart. Whatever the outcome, I was going to kiss him at midnight. And if the coach turned back into a pumpkin, then the fairytale in my head was over.

As the audience in Times Square counted down with Dick Clark, the ball slowly dropped, and my heart raced inside my chest. My breath stuck in my throat. I was really going to do it. I was going to kiss my best friend. The countdown stopped at zero. And the ball finished dropping.

"Cowboy," I whispered.

He turned his head. I stared into his big, light-blue eyes. Resting my hands on his cheeks, I pushed my lips onto his before I could talk myself out of it. I wasn't sure if the fireworks popping off in my ears were from the kiss or the TV. My lips sparked like a sparkler.

The kiss ended before I was ready. I slowly opened my eyes. Wyatt was staring at me. I wasn't sure if that was a good thing or a bad one. "Um . . . I should . . . um . . . get goin'. I have chores to do in a few hours," he stammered as he tripped over the arm of the couch and raced out the door.

My heart sank to the floor as the tears followed its trail. They fell like a torrential rainfall. *I blew it! Caitlyn, why did you do that?* I scoffed at myself before turning off the TV and stomping to my room.

Chapter 18

Wyatt

I raced out of Caitlyn's cabin, my heart beating out of my chest. *Why'd she do that?* I'd never been kissed before. Not on my lips anyway. I pressed my fingertips to my still-tingling lips.

Scurrying over to my cabin, I didn't take a breath until I was safe and sound behind the locked door. Leaning against the strong wood door, my chest heaved as I tried to take in air.

Why did you run away, you idiot? I had no idea how to answer that question. All I knew was that I was the biggest idiot ever. The only girl I'd ever loved had kissed me, and I ran away.

I closed my eyes and tapped my head against the door. *Wyatt, you are stupid, stupid, stupid.* I had no idea if she would ever talk to me again. If she didn't, my heart would never recover. And it would be all my fault.

* * *

The next morning, I was slow to wake. My heart was heavy. I wanted to stay in bed and never go out again. Avoid the world. Avoid the heartache of Caitlyn not talking to me ever again. But there were chores to be done. The horses didn't need to suffer because of my stupidity. I groaned and rolled out of bed.

After pulling on my jeans and buttoning my green plaid shirt, I slipped on my boots, plopped my hat on my head, and traipsed down to the stable. As I approached the stable doors, I heard voices. The male voice belonged to Luke. "Please, Caitlyn. I could really use your help," he was saying.

My heart thudded in my chest. It wasn't like me to feel jealous, especially of Luke since I knew he loved Emelia. But it was there anyway. I didn't like it.

Caitlyn sighed. "Okay. Sure."

"Thank you. Thank you. But please keep it a secret. I owe ya one."

When I heard Luke's footsteps, I took a deep breath and held it as I stepped inside. "Mornin'." I did my best to sound confident.

Caitlyn was raking out one of the stalls, and she jumped at the sound of my voice. "Hey," she responded awkwardly without turning around.

Yep. I blew it. "Are ya tryin' to replace me?" I chuckled.

She turned around, her eyes wide. "What do ya mean?"

I motioned toward the rake. "Well, that there is my job."

"I'm . . . I'm sorry. I just wanted to make myself useful. Classes don't start until next week." She held out the rake.

"How 'bout we work together? I'll start at this end." I pointed toward the opposite end of the stable. "And we can meet in the middle."

She flashed the briefest of half smiles. "Sure." Then, she turned back to the stall.

"Chipmunk . . ." I reached out my hand to her.

She glanced over her shoulder. "Yeah?"

I opened my mouth to apologize for running out. "Thanks for your help." *You idiot!*

Turning, I grabbed a rake and dragged it to the opposite end of the stable. I sighed and slapped the bottom of the rake on a pile of hay.

What can I do to make it up to her? Valentine's Day is in a month. Maybe I can come up with somethin'. But I can't wait that long to apologize to her. UGH! What am I gonna do? I do want to give her the best Valentine's Day she's ever had, though. She deserves it. I'll think of somethin' before then. My heart can't handle this.

Maybe we could go for a ride on Flash and Minnie, and we could talk. Finally tell her how I feel about her. Maybe we could go out for dinner. I sighed and hung my head.

Feeling defeated, I glanced at my watch. *Lunch time.* I set the rake against the stall's wall. As I stepped into the main stable area, I noticed Caitlyn had already finished and left. I still had one stall left to do. I guess all of my thinking made me work slower. Pain jabbed at my heart. I'd really screwed up.

My shoulders slumped as my heart fell to the bottom of my stomach. I was going to go to the house for lunch, but I turned toward my cabin instead. I wasn't in the mood for company.

I trudged up the path to my cabin. My legs felt as heavy as lead. As I crested the top of the hill, I was just in time to see Caitlyn disappear inside her own cabin. Sighing heavily, I continued with the last few steps to my door and went inside.

I miss her so much already. God, how do I fix this? I guess all I can really do is apologize.

Go to her. Tell her.

Turning around, I grabbed the doorknob and yanked the door back open. I marched across the road, gravel crunching under my feet. Holding my breath, I knocked on Caitlyn's door. The moments before she opened the door felt like an eternity. As the door crept open—in slow motion it seemed—I let out the breath until there was nothing left in my lungs.

Caitlyn's eyes grew wide before quickly going back to normal. "Hey, Cowboy."

At least she hasn't resorted to callin' me by my first name. Maybe there's still a chance, then.

She twisted the cuffs of her shirt sleeves in her hands. "What's up?"

"Nothin'." My voice was barely audible. I cleared my throat. "I miss my best friend. I'm really sorry for runnin' out after you kissed me. I was just caught off guard. Could we just forget I ever did that?"

She crossed her arms over her chest. "Then, why did ya?"

My eyes fell to the ground. I massaged the back of my neck. *Oh, man. She's not gonna make this easy, is she?* "Honestly, I got scared." My face felt like it was on fire. "I've never been kissed before. Not on the lips anyway." I swallowed the lump in my throat as I raised my eyes to meet hers.

Caitlyn's eyes widened in realization of what I'd confessed. "You haven't?"

"No." My eyes fell to my feet as I ran my boot over a rock lodged between the slats on her porch.

"I haven't either." She shrugged. "We can forget it happened, if ya want to."

I stuffed my hands deep into my front pockets. "Would ya wanna take Minnie and Flash for a ride?"

Her face lit up. "Yes! I didn't get to take her for one yesterday like I'd wanted." She pulled her jacket from the hook inside her door and stepped outside, closing the door behind her. "Let's go."

The silence between us was still there as we headed back down the hill to the horses. At least it was less awkward than before. After saddling up Minnie and Flash, we headed toward the trees on the other side of the cabins. We had spent the weekend between Christmas and New Year's taking down the lights and Christmas decorations.

"So . . . I overheard you and Luke talkin' earlier. What was that about? Somethin' 'bout a secret?"

"Oh . . . um . . ." She sighed. "He just wants help with a surprise for Emelia."

"That's cool." I wanted to know but wasn't about to press my luck about it.

I inhaled a deep breath of the crisp January air. Every time I came out riding, I loved the place more and more. If that was even possible. But never more than I loved the girl next to me. I needed to tell her, but every time I got the courage, my tongue became dry and the words got stuck in my throat. Or someone was always interrupting.

Now that she's here to stay, if I tell her I'm in love with her, will I still be holdin' her back? Or will I lose her forever? She did kiss me, though. But maybe she didn't mean it. Maybe she just wanted to see what it was like.

I peeked at Caitlyn out of the corner of my eye. She appeared to be lost in her own thoughts. I took those few precious moments to study her. Her long blonde hair blew gently in the air and across her face. Her bright, blue eyes—just a shade darker than mine—were staring off into the distance.

Caitlyn's eyes shifted and met mine as her cheeks grew red. "What?"

"I love you, Caitlyn Logan." The words flew out of my mouth before my mind could even process them. *What? No! Not like that!*

"That's sweet, Wyatt Glover. I love you, too."

"No, Chipmunk. I'm *in* love with you. I have been since the day we met in the middle of the living room at Colt's house."

Heat rushed to my face, and my heart was about to pop.

Understanding washed over her face. "Oh, Cowboy. You deserve so much better than me. You deserve someone who is healthy and who you won't have to take care of."

"Shouldn't that be *my* decision? *My* choice?"

Caitlyn swiped away a tear that had fallen to her cheek. "I'm sorry. I really gotta go." She grabbed hold of the reins and turned Minnie toward the stable before trotting off.

"Chipmunk!" I yelled after her. I patted Flash on the neck. "Well, that went about like I thought it would. I've pretty much lost her at this point, Flash. Doesn't she know there isn't anyone better than her? Doesn't she know she's the *only* one for me?" Tears pricked my eyes.

Let her go. For now. My time, My son. All in My time.

I lifted my face to heaven and closed my eyes. *Okay, God. I trust you.*

"Let's head back, Flash." I pulled on the reins, and Flash turned in the direction I wanted him to go. The heaviness of his hooves hitting the ground matched the weight of sadness in my heart.

I held my breath as I led Flash into the stable. I wasn't sure if Caitlyn would still be there or not. Colt appeared to be the only one inside. He slid the saddle off Minnie and flopped it onto the sawhorse next to him.

Colt glanced over his shoulder. "Hey, Wyatt. What happened with Caitlyn?"

I turned to undo the saddle buckles. "Uh . . . why do ya ask?"

In my peripheral vision, Colt faced me with his hands on his waist. "Well, Caitlyn brought Minnie in here with a tear-stained face, handed me the reins, and high-tailed it outta here."

Closing my eyes, I pressed my fingertips to the bridge of my nose. My head started to pound. "Well . . . last night, she kissed me, and I ran out on her. Today, I told her I am in love with her, and *she* ran away from *me*."

Colt stepped closer, cocking his ear toward me. "Y'all did what now?"

"You heard me." I blew out a breath.

"Well, it's about time." He slapped me on the shoulder. "What happened?"

I lowered my gaze to the ground. "She said I deserve a woman who is healthy; one I don't have to take care of. And then, she ran away. I didn't mean to just blurt it out the way I did. The words were out of my mouth before my mind could stop them."

"Aww, Wyatt. I'm so sorry." He squeezed my shoulder. "Give her some time to let it set in. She's in love with you, too. She's just not ready to admit it yet."

I sighed. "It's all in God's hands now. I don't know what else to do. I had a plan for Valentine's Day . . . sort of. But it looks like it might be dead in the water."

Colt swiped his index finger across his bottom lip. "No. No. Keep your plan. I'll make sure she's there."

"Well, I haven't actually thought it all out yet."

"I'll help ya. Don't lose hope."

"Hope and faith that God will work it out are really all I have." I shrugged.

Chapter 19

Caitlyn

"**A**re ya ready to help me plan this for Emelia?" Luke asked me in a hushed voice as we stood outside the paddock, watching a horse run around the inside. An owner had tied her to a tree on the ranch during the night. I thought people only did that with dogs outside of shelters. Either way, it was too cruel.

"Yeah. I'm ready."

Not really. The last thing I wanted to do was help Luke with a romantic gesture. Wyatt had been scarce since the debacle I made of his confession of his love for me. It had been a few weeks since then. I didn't know if we had been avoiding each other or if we were both busy, so it kept us apart. EMT classes had started, and they were keeping me busy with them being mostly in Elizabeth City, which was about forty minutes away.

"What do ya think Uncle Colt is gonna do with her?" I nodded toward the mare. She was all white. Not a speck of color on her except on her hooves and the top of her nose. She was like a ghost. As I twisted my snowflake pendant in my fingers, her name came to me. "Winter's Whisper."

"What's that?" Luke asked.

"Her name should be Winter's Whisper." I smiled.

"That sounds like a fine name for her," Uncle Colt chimed

in from behind us.

My smile grew. "Really?"

"Sure. You haven't had the chance to name a horse yet. So, why not? Winter's Whisper it is." He glanced at the horse in the paddock. "It suits her, I think."

"Ya ready, Caitlyn?" Luke asked.

"Yep."

As we walked to the stable, Luke ran through his idea for Valentine's Day. "So, I was thinkin' a candlelit dinner at our favorite spot by the water. Okay, it's *my* favorite spot, but I know she'll love it. It's the picnic table between the two trees by the lighthouse."

"Oh, I love that spot."

"I'll get dinner from The Herring House restaurant. We'll be able to hear the live music they usually have. And after we've finished with dessert, I'll ask her with this." He pulled a small black box from his pocket and opened it.

I gasped. "Oh, Luke. This is gorgeous! She's going to *love* this."

"Ya really think so? It's not dorky that it's in the shape of a heart?" He bit his bottom lip and peered down at me.

"It's perfect, Luke. Truly."

"Thanks. So, how do you like the plan?" Hope glinted in his eyes.

"It sounds like a perfect and romantic evening for a proposal. She's going to love it. Guess ya didn't really need my help after all." I laughed.

"Well, I needed your opinion. And if your opinion was that it wasn't a good plan, then, yes, I was goin' ta need all the help I could get." He chuckled.

"Well, glad I could be of assistance. I'm gonna head back out and watch the horse. She's gorgeous, isn't she?" I pointed my thumb over my shoulder.

"That she is."

"Good luck, Luke."

"Thanks. I'm gonna need it."

"You won't need luck. She loves you. She's goin' to say yes." I smiled as I turned and headed back to the paddock.

* * *

I woke up to a heaviness in my chest. Had a Mack truck hit me overnight? The pressure in my head felt like a vice was squeezing it. My mouth was like cotton and my throat like sandpaper. I groaned. *It's Valentine's Day.* I'd missed the last couple of days of classes because I wasn't feeling well and was struggling to keep my blood sugar under control.

I rolled out of bed and went to the kitchen for a glass of water. I measured out my insulin before shooting it into my stomach. My blood sugar was on the rise. Again.

I sighed and threw on some sweats and laced up my sneakers. Exercise sometimes helped lower my blood sugar, so I decided to walk down to the stable. Warrior and Minnie would make me feel better. Maybe I'd even take Minnie for a stroll.

As I slowly made my way down the path to the stable, I breathed in and out as steadily as I could. When I finally arrived at the stable door, Warrior appeared at the door of his stall.

My head felt light. Nausea plagued me just before the contents of my stomach flew from my lips. Everything became blurry. *What's going on? Uncle Colt! Cowboy . . .*

Chapter 20

Wyatt

As I was in the corral tending to Minnie and Flash, Warrior's frantic cries echoed from the stable. He hadn't made that kind of sound since Callie got bit by that Copperhead. My eyes widened as it hit me. *Somethin's not right.*

Remembering I saw Caitlyn as she passed by the corral a few minutes before, I bolted in that direction as fast as my legs would carry me. I stood in the back doorway, my eyes frantically searching to see what had gotten into Warrior. My eyes landed on the ground in front of his stall. Caitlyn was lying there, her body lifeless.

I ran and slid to the ground next to Caitlyn. "Chipmunk! Chipmunk!" My breath lodged in my throat. I swallowed hard, choking down my emotions. My heart thumped rapidly.

When she didn't respond, I floundered to get my phone out of my pocket. It hit the ground, causing a dust cloud to rise all around it. I let out a frustrated growl as I scrambled to pick it up. My chubby fingers struggled to dial 9-1-1.

"Chowan County 9-1-1. What's your emergency?"

"Yes, I need an ambulance at Redemption Ranch." I struggled to remember the address.

"I need your location, sir."

"336 Redemption Drive," I all but shouted into the phone.

"Please hurry!"

"Okay, sir. Take a deep breath. I need to know the nature of the emergency so I can relay it to the paramedics."

I breathed in deeply and steadied my voice. "It's Caitlyn Logan. She's unconscious."

"Is she breathing? Does she have a pulse?"

I checked for her pulse and watched to see if her chest rose and fell. "Yes, barely. She's got type 1 diabetes."

"Help is on the way. Stay on the line with me until they arrive."

"Yes, ma'am. Chipmunk, wake up! Please, wake up!" I pleaded with her. Tears dripped to my cheeks.

Caitlyn's lifeless body lying in my arms was one of the worst things I'd ever witnessed in my life. I'd never been more terrified. Not even when I realized my parents had abandoned me. I flicked my eyes up to heaven. "Please, Lord. Don't take her. Please."

Footsteps sounded behind me.

"What's goin' on?" Colt asked. "What happened?" He kneeled beside me.

"I don't know." Tears flowed freely, strangling my words. "I heard Warrior's frantic cries and came to see what was wrong. This is how I found her." My body shook with emotion. I rocked back and forth, willing the ambulance to come faster.

"We need to get her to the hospital." Colt paced back and forth.

"I'm on the line with 9-1-1 right now. Ambulance is on the way."

"Tell them to hurry up!" Colt growled.

I heard the sirens in the distance, growing louder as they drew closer.

"I'll go meet them." Colt sprinted outside.

It took what seemed like forever before the paramedics rushed through the door. "What happened?" the first one asked.

I scurried out of their way. "Uh . . ." Again, my words struggled to be free. "I found her like this. She's barely breathing and barely has a pulse. She has type 1 diabetes, so I'm not sure if that has anything to do with what happened or not. I was going to check her blood sugar, but I can't find her phone."

"I'm goin' ta call Marci and Chuck so they can meet the ambulance at the hospital." Colt bolted out with his phone to his ear.

"Let's get some oxygen going," the first paramedic told the second.

The second paramedic took out a mask with a bag attached to it and placed it over Caitlyn's mouth and nose.

The first paramedic, who had *Stevens* stitched onto his uniform, pricked Caitlyn's finger to check her blood sugar. I only knew about this because I had seen Caitlyn do it a million times before she got the reader on her arm. He squeezed some blood onto a test strip and inserted it into the reader he'd pulled from his bag beside him.

The second paramedic, with *Anderson* on her uniform, said, "Her blood pressure is 80 over 50."

The reader beeped, and Stevens reported, "Her blood sugar is 350. I'm goin' to start an IV of insulin."

Everything they did and said was in slow motion. "Can't you go any faster?" I pleaded.

"Sir, we are doin' what we need to do in order to transport her to the hospital while treatin' her as fast as possible. Now, if you could step back and let us do our job," Stevens commanded.

"I'm sorry." I ran my hands through my hair and interlaced them at my neck as I moved away from them.

After the IV was in and working, they lifted Caitlyn's still-motionless body onto the gurney. "You're welcome to ride with us if ya want," Anderson offered.

"Thank you." I fell into step behind them. After they pushed the gurney into the back of the ambulance, I hoisted myself inside and slid onto the bench seat.

"Her levels are extremely high," Stevens mentioned as the ambulance pulled away from the stable. "Has she mentioned anythin' to you? Maybe she ate without takin' her insulin or has been sick?"

"We haven't talked in a couple of weeks, so I'm not sure." My heart plunged to my stomach. *Has it really been that long since we talked?*

Things hadn't been the same since I blurted out my feelings for Caitlyn. If I were being honest with myself, things hadn't been the same since I ran out after she kissed me. Now, if anything happened to her, I'd never forgive myself for leaving things the way I did.

Alarms started sounding, ringing in my ears. "What's that? What's happenin'?"

"She's coding!" Stevens shouted as he put two pads on Caitlyn's body.

I felt the ambulance speed up as he grabbed a machine and removed two paddles. My eyes were as wide as saucers as I knew exactly what that machine was for. My heart leapt to my throat. Her heart had stopped beating.

No, God! No! Please don't take her! Take me if you have to take someone!

"Clear!" Stevens shocked her body, and it convulsed upward. "Still nothing! Charging . . . Clear!" He shocked her once more. Again, her body contorted in the air.

Finally, the machine started beeping again. I let out a long, slow, ragged breath. I closed my eyes. *Thank you, Jesus. Thank you.*

Chapter 21

Caitlyn

As the light lit up my eyelids, I slowly lifted them. "What happened?" A blaring white light blinded me. I lifted my arm to shield my eyes. When the light dimmed, I expected to be standing in front of Warrior. But I was standing in a field. "How did I get here? Where am I?" I was facing a pond that seemed familiar but couldn't quite figure out why.

Three figures were standing on the dock. They were fuzzy, so I cautiously made my way over to them. "Maybe they can tell me where I am." I could make out that all three figures were men, but I still wasn't sure if I knew them or not.

My brows furrowed in confusion. Is that? No . . . it can't be. "Grandpa Heidlage? Uncle Mark? Uncle Bob?" I raced the rest of the way to them. When they turned around, my cheeks were showered with tears. "What are ya doin' here?"

"We were told to come here and wait for a visitor," Grandpa informed me.

"Wait . . . you're all . . . Am I . . . ?" I patted my body as if that would answer the question I couldn't quite bring myself to finish.

They all chuckled like I'd just told the best joke.

"No. No, you're not," Grandpa responded.

"Then, how am I here . . . with you?" Panic bubbled up

from the pit of my stomach.

Uncle Bob placed his hand on my shoulder, and calmness washed over me. "Well, you're in a coma. So, you're kinda stuck between here and there."

It felt so weird. That was a hard pill to swallow. It was like I was in my body, but I wasn't. "I've missed you all so much!" I lunged forward with my arms wide open. Feeling their embrace after so many years filled my heart and sent peace spiraling through my body. "Can we sit? I'm feelin' a little tired."

"Of course." Grandpa held my hand as I sat down on the end of the dock.

All three of them joined me, dangling our feet above the dark, murky water.

"I woulda thought the water here would be prettier." I shrugged.

Grandpa chuckled.

"So, what's with this boy Wyatt?" Uncle Mark asked after a few seconds of silence.

"Wow. Way to be nonchalant about it, Mark." Uncle Bob elbowed him in the arm.

"Well, we were all thinkin' it and have been." Uncle Mark tossed his hands in the air.

"What do ya mean?" I shrugged again. "He's just my best friend. At least he was."

"We all know that's not entirely true." Grandpa poked me in the side with his index finger.

"Yeah, he told you he's in love with you a few weeks ago, didn't he?" Uncle Bob chimed in again. "And he was goin' to ask ya to dinner on Valentine's Day."

"He was? How'd you . . ." I raised a shoulder to my cheek. "We always hang out on Valentine's Day, though."

"Yeah, but what about his feelin's for you, and yours for him?" Uncle Mark asked. "Doesn't that make it a little different this year?"

I scratched my head as I pondered his question. "I suppose so."

"And we all know you don't love each other as just best friends," Uncle Bob teased.

My cheeks heated up, and it wasn't because of the bright sun overhead. "And what if we do? I can't ask him to deal with all of this for the rest of his life. It's just too much, and he deserves better than that. Especially after the life he's had." I swiped at a tear that had fallen to my cheek as Grandpa took my hand in his.

"You need to tell him you feel the same way he does," Grandpa said. "Let him decide if it's too much. True love doesn't come with limits, Caitlyn, sweetheart. True love is takin' those limitations and lovin' the person in spite of them. No matter what. Lovin' without limits is the best kind of love and the greatest treasure. You, of all people, know how fleetin' life is. Tell him while you still have a chance to." He kissed the temple of my head and released my hand.

"Thanks, Grandpa."

When I moved my gaze from the water to where they were, they were gone. "No! I need more time with them!" New tears trickled down my cheeks. Never enough time. I sat in silence on the dock, thinking about what Grandpa had said.

"What if Cowboy doesn't feel the same about me? I mean, he did tell me he's in love with me. But what if I tell him I feel the same, and he's changed his mind?" I couldn't go the rest of my life without him in it. The few weeks we hadn't talked were torture enough. I lifted my face to the sky. "Lord, what do I do?"

Rest in Me. I am always with you. My will be done on Earth as it is in Heaven.

I lay on the dock, staring up at the bright blue sky as peace like I'd never felt before enveloped me like a warm hug. I inhaled deeply as the breeze blew scents of fragrant flowers over me. I knew in that moment that I'd tell Wyatt how I really felt about him. If it were in God's will for us to be together, as more than best friends, it would be. I just had to figure out how to get out of here.

Chapter 22

Wyatt

With a giant lump in my throat, I stepped gingerly into the hospital room in the Intensive Care Unit. I glanced at the bed. Caitlyn still looked the same. Her eyes were closed. What I would have given to see those bright blue eyes again. My heart sank. *Oh, my sweet, sweet Chipmunk.*

The whirring of a machine caught my attention. I followed the cords that slid under the blanket. They were somehow attached to her body. What the machine did, I had no clue.

My eyes eventually landed on Caitlyn's mom. Her eyes were puffy with dark circles underneath. They weren't as bright as they usually were. Her hair was in a messy bun resting on top of her head. She sat in a chair and was holding Caitlyn's hand.

"Hey, Mrs. Logan. Any change?" I asked just above a whisper.

"Oh, hey, Wyatt." She uncrossed her legs and let go of Caitlyn's hand to wipe hers down her pant leg. "They said she made great strides overnight with her lungs. Their biggest concern now is her kidney function and brain healing. They aren't sure if she'll have to do dialysis or not. Just depends on if her kidneys improve." Mrs. Logan sucked in a deep breath and let it out slowly. Her eyes were glassy. "We won't know anythin' about her brain until they are able to wean her off sedation, which they are goin' to start doin' slowly in the mornin'."

"I'm sorry I couldn't be here earlier. I wish I could be here all the time." I sighed as I choked back tears.

Mrs. Logan stood from her chair and patted my hand that was resting on the white metal bed frame. "Well, you're here now. That's what matters. I'm goin' to call the pastor and let him know what's goin' on. Will you sit with her?"

"Of course."

"Thank you, Wyatt." She wrapped her arms around me, catching me off guard.

Before I had the chance to return the hug, she was out the door. I sat down in the brown chair that was now empty, afraid to touch Caitlyn. There were tubes everywhere and machines beeping, echoing in my ears. The only machine I knew was the one counting her heartbeats. I stared at the numbers on the monitor until they blurred. I placed my hand on the bed next to hers and inched my index finger closer to her hand, barely grazing her pinky.

"God, I don't know what you're doin', but please don't take her away before I have her. I know, now, that I wasted so much time." I swiped at a tear that dripped down my cheek and landed on the blanket. I cleared my throat. "I was trapped in my fear and didn't tell her exactly how I feel. But you saw what happened when I did. I know this can't be the end of her life or the end of our story. It just can't be. It's all in Your hands now, God. Your will be done."

I rested my head on my arm and closed my eyes, the silence deafening. Except for the beeping. And I waited. Waited on God. And waited on Caitlyn.

Chapter 23

Caitlyn

Childlike giggles sounded from behind me. I turned in that direction. A small figure bounded toward me. As it came closer, the figure became clearer.

"No way! Quinnie Bear?" I jumped to my feet and whispered to myself. "It can't be. Quinn!"

I ran as fast as my feet would go toward her. She was dressed just as she would have been on Earth. She was wearing a light pink sundress, her hair in pigtail braids—her favorite—and those pink cowgirl boots Luke had given her. She adored those boots.

"Caitlyn!" She squeezed my neck.

"What are you doin' here?" I asked as I set her on her feet. The wetness from her cheeks glistened in the sunlight. I had no idea if it was from my tears or her's or both.

Quinn swiped a finger across my cheeks. "What's wrong, Caitlyn? Aren't you happy to see me?"

"Oh, yes. I'm so happy to see you, Quinn. I've missed you so much!" I wrapped her in my arms once more. Then, I pulled away from her. "Wait! You said Caitlyn! You can pronounce your 'L' now!"

"Yep!" She nodded proudly, causing her curls at the end of her braids to bounce against her shoulders. "God said I could

come and see you. And I couldn't not come see you! But why are you here? Are you dead like me?" Her brows narrowed.

"No. I don't think so. I guess I'm in a coma. Stuck between here and there." That sounded so weird to say.

"Oh." She hung her head. "I'm sorry."

We sat in a field of vibrant wildflowers. There were so many colors and different scents wafting through the air. Everything here—wherever here was—was more colorful and brighter, and the smells were stronger and bolder.

"No. I should be the one apologizin' to you."

"For what?" Her voice lifted.

"I'm sorry I wasn't at the fair to protect you that night." I pulled Quinn onto my lap.

"It's okay." Quinn pulled at a flower as a single tear slid down her cheek. "I miss Mommy. And Luke. And Colt. And Callie. And Tinkerbell. And Wyatt. And you." Her lip trembled.

"I know you do. I'm so sorry. We all miss you, too. So much." I stroked the ends of her braids.

"God said I needed to be here with Him, so that Mommy could be here with Him, too, when it's time. I do like it here, though. Are you going to stay here with me?" She glanced up at me with her sparkling green eyes. They were brighter than I'd ever seen them.

"I'm not sure. I'll stay as long as God lets me, though."

"If you go back, will you tell Mommy and Luke that I love them as big as the sky and miss them just as much? And that I'm okay up here, too? And tell Tinkerbell, too?"

I squeezed her close. My heart felt as if it might burst. I closed my eyes and inhaled her rose-scented hair. Just like I remembered. "I love you, Quinnie Bear. I miss you so much!"

"I love you, too." Her voice sounded off in the distance instead of right in front of me.

When I opened my eyes, my arms were empty. I wrapped them around myself as my body shook with grief, my heart shattered one more time. I needed more time. With all of them.

I fell into the depths of the darkness. Like Alice in Wonderland. But I wasn't falling, and I wasn't landing anywhere. I was just there. In the darkness. Alone.

You are never alone. I am always with you.

"No! I'm not ready to leave! Please!" I reached out into the darkness, grasping for anything I could get my hands on but came up empty.

Chapter 24

Wyatt

"**W**yatt! Wyatt!"

My body jerked forward and then backward. I opened my eyes. Colt was standing next to me with his hand resting on my shoulder. I rubbed the sleep from my eyes. "I guess I fell asleep?" I sat up and stretched my back.

"Apparently. Why don't we go to the cafeteria and get somethin' ta eat?"

Tears sprang to my eyes, and my voice cracked. "Why? I don't wanna leave her, Colt. What if she wakes up, and I'm not here?"

"I know, but the doctor needs to come in and talk with Marci and Chuck."

I sighed. "Okay."

As we made our way down the hallway, I said, "It's been two weeks, Colt. I'm worried. What if she doesn't wake up? I can't take losin' another person in my life." I swiped my nose with my shirt sleeve.

Colt wrapped his hand around the back of my neck. "I know. I'm worried, too. But God's got this. We all have to believe that. Marci and Chuck do with every fiber of their bein'."

"I do. Or at least I'm tryin' to. Faith as small as mouse

poop, right?" I softly chuckled as Quinn's face flashed through my mind.

"Exactly." Colt smiled.

After we finished eating, I said, "I'm gonna go spend some time in the chapel."

"Sounds like a good place to be."

I made my way down the long, white hallway. The smell of antiseptic burned into my nose. My footsteps echoed through the silence.

Slowly dragging open the heavy door with a sign indicating the chapel was on the other side, I stepped inside. Walking down the narrow aisle, my boots scuffed on the carpet. I slid into a pew in the second row. There was a cross in front of a stained-glass window. The stained glass cast a soft glow in an array of colors down the main aisle. I stared at the cross. I had no idea how to put into words the thoughts that were stabbing at my heart.

"God, I don't know where to start. I'm feeling so many different emotions at the same time. Please don't take her." I lowered my head as the tears fell from my eyes, and my shoulders shook, releasing every one of those emotions to Him. "I have so much I still want to say to her. To experience with her. I know that if it's in Your will, she will wake up. Help me keep my faith, Father God."

I sucked in a deep breath. I sat talking to God silently, waiting for Him to answer. If He *was* going to answer.

"Anythin' I can pray with you about, son?" I jumped as I wasn't expecting anyone else to be there. A hand touched my shoulder as a bald, stout man sat next to me. I assumed he was the hospital chaplain.

"Oh. Um. My friend." I coughed. "My best friend is in a coma. Just prayin' that God won't take her. I'd sacrifice myself if it meant she could stay here."

"Oh, son. God doesn't want that. God's will is God's will."

"I know." I deeply sighed. "But we just lost Quinn. I don't think anyone could handle another loss like that."

"Second Corinthians Chapter four, verses 17 and 18 say, 'For our light and momentary troubles are achieving for us an eternal glory that far outweighs them all. So, we fix our eyes not on what is seen, but on what is unseen, since what is seen is temporary, but what is unseen is eternal.' Keep your eyes on God. He will show you the way." The man quietly stood and treaded out the door, leaving me to figure out what he actually meant.

"Just please don't take my girl, God. Please," I whispered to the cross before standing and plodding out of the chapel.

I stuffed my hands in my pockets and headed back to Caitlyn's room. Muffled voices could be heard as I made my way down the hall. It wasn't until I was closer to her room that I realized that's where they were coming from.

"She has been responding to intentional stimuli, which is good because it means her brain stem is healing. We were also able to finally find a pulse in her right foot. Those are all signs of her body healing. She isn't out of the woods yet, but she is closer than she was yesterday."

"Thank you, Dr. Wilson. We serve an amazin' God who is workin' miracles," Mrs. Logan told him.

"Yes. Yes, we most certainly do. Caitlyn is a fighter. I haven't seen this kind of turnaround from anyone in her condition. But we still need to prepare for the worst-case scenario."

"Thanks, Doc," Mr. Logan said. "But we serve a mighty God, like my wife said. The Master Physician."

Silence filled the room before the doctor strode past me, his white coat billowing at his sides as he moved down the hallway.

I stood in the doorway for a second before lightly knocking. "So, good news and bad news, huh?"

"Oh, Wyatt. We have to believe that God has a plan and will heal our sweet girl." Mrs. Logan hugged me. "Thy will be done."

"I hope one day I can have your kind of faith. I strive to every day, but I feel so helpless."

"Honey, it's when we feel the most helpless that we have to reach out and lean on God the most. Lean not on our own understandin', but on His, and His alone."

My throat tightened as emotion threatened to overtake me. I nodded.

"We'll give ya some time with her." Mr. Logan patted my shoulder.

I nodded in his direction, not trusting my voice to speak.

Once they left the room, I fell to the chair beside the bed. I wasn't fearful of touching Caitlyn anymore. I needed to feel her hand. I latched onto her hand with both of mine. I wanted . . . no, I *needed* her to know I was there. One hundred percent, without a doubt. I needed her to know that I would always be there for her. No matter what.

Fight to come back to me, Chipmunk. Fight hard. I love you with every fiber of my bein', and I want to make sure you know that and know that I'm not goin' anywhere. Ever.

Chapter 25

Caitlyn

"God, I know I'm still new at this."

It took me a minute to figure out the voice in the darkness. It was a female voice. But not Mom's. Or Aunt Callie's. Maybe Emelia?

I tried as hard as I could to open my eyes. But it was like they'd been glued shut. "Why won't they open?" The faint glow of light teased me from behind my eyelids.

The voice continued, "But if You are who You say You are, please let her wake up. I can't lose her, too. I'm trying my best to have faith, but this is all still so new. I do know You don't work this way, but I need a miracle to solidify my faith. Please, God. Hear my plea."

It was definitely Emelia's voice. My hand lifted off the bed and was surrounded by two hands. I tried my hardest to squeeze her hand.

Warmth and peace engulfed me once again. My body tingled all over. I tried to move and open my eyes, but everything was pinned down. That's what it felt like anyway.

"God, why can't I wake up? I just want to wake up and hug my mom and dad. And Dyl. And Cowboy. Everyone. Please!" I begged.

Was God testing my faith? Was this what was meant when

Peter wrote, "So that the tested genuine as of your faith—of greater worth than gold, which perishes even though refined by fire—may result in praise, glory, and honor when Jesus Christ is revealed?"

Is this going to bring You glory and honor and praise, God? Are You using me to bring people closer to You? I'm not ready to die.

My peace be with you. Abide in Me, and I will give you the desires of your heart.

Always, God. Your ways are not my own.

Chapter 26

Wyatt

"It's been four weeks, Chipmunk. Four weeks since I saw your big, beautiful blue eyes. Four weeks since I've heard your sweet voice and witnessed your wonderful smile." I wiped the side of my eye where a tear had formed. "The doctor said your body is healed, more than they could have predicted. He said we just have to wait for you to wake up. He said he's goin' to take you completely off sedation and the ventilator tomorrow. I sure hope you wake up after that. We all do."

I glanced up at the white, round clock hanging on the wall and sighed. "Visitin' hours are over, so I'd best get out of here before they kick me out. I'm sure they're tired of doin' that. But I'll be back tomorrow. I promise."

I stood over Caitlyn and kissed her forehead before whispering in her ear, "I love you, Caitlyn LeeAnn Logan. I always have, and I always will. You've had my heart since day one, Chipmunk. You'll have it till my last."

I planted my lips gently on her cheek before leaving the room.

* * *

The next morning was Sunday, March 16. Instead of heading to the hospital, I drove to church. In that moment, I felt that was where I needed to be. In the house of the Lord, worshipping His goodness, His mercy, and His grace. I knew I wouldn't be able to be in the room when they were removing the ventilator anyway. So, the best place for me to be was in church.

That morning, I sat in the front of the sanctuary. I was feeling so lost and empty and helpless. I needed God more that day than I ever had before.

The worship band started with an upbeat song. It did nothing for my soul, though. I needed a worship song. One that hit me straight in the heart.

Ask and ye shall receive. As the band began to play the next song, I knew the song from the first note played. One of my favorites: "He Will Carry Me" by Mark Schultz. Tears welled in my eyes as my knees hit the floor, and my arms rose to heaven.

God, I know You can hear me. "Chipmunk's body is battered and broken. I know You are with her. Wrap Your loving arms around her, God. Let Your love be a big comfort to her and the Logan family. And all of us who love her. My heart is wounded without her, Lord. You are my strength in this storm." My arms shook in the air, and tears drowned my face.

"Heal Caitlyn's body, mind, and spirit, Father God. If that means on the other side of heaven, so be it. I beg you, though, for her parents' sake and my own, let it be *this* side of heaven." I shook my fists toward the ceiling. "No matter what, God, we will love You. We will honor You, and we will praise Your holy name. You will always carry us. In Jesus's mighty name. Amen."

When my mind returned to where I was, the church was so

silent you could hear a pin drop. On the carpet, even. I opened my eyes. I was surrounded by the entire congregation. Hands were on my shoulders, my head, and my back. There wasn't a single face that wasn't stained with tears. I hadn't even realized I'd said my prayer out loud, let alone loud enough for it to disrupt worship.

As I lowered my hands and raised myself to standing, my phone vibrated in my back pocket. I looked at the notification on my lock screen. A text from Mrs. Logan. My heart stopped. With shaking hands, I opened the message. I closed my eyes. *Please, God.*

She's awake! Praise God! She's awake!

I fell back to my knees in the middle of the aisle and sobbed. *Thank you, Jesus!* I held my phone in the air and shouted, "She's awake!"

Applause erupted, and the band made a joyful noise. Hands were raised in the air, and shouts of praise filled the room.

"I gotta go!" I wiped my eyes with the backs of my hands as I stood. I tried to run at the same time and tripped over my feet. It didn't stop me from bolting out of the church like it was on fire. "I gotta go! She's awake!"

Chapter 27

Caitlyn

I swallowed hard, my throat raw and on fire from the tube. "Mom," I said, my voice raspy. "Where's Wyatt? And Emelia?" I took a sip of water, but it was like swallowing shards of glass. "I have so much to tell you, Mom."

Mom's face twisted in confusion. "What do you mean? You've been in a coma for four weeks. What could you possibly have to tell me?"

"I don't know, Mom. It was the weirdest thing. I remember passing out in the stable while I was talkin' to Warrior. When my eyes opened again, I was in this field near a pond. There was a dock, and three figures were standin' there. It was Grandpa, Uncle Mark, and Uncle Bob, Mom." Tears sprinkled my cheeks. "I sat there and talked with them for quite a while. They had some good advice for me. Mostly about Wyatt. But I got to hug them and talk to them. It was wonderful." Heat burned my cheeks. I coughed.

Mom's eyes became glassy. She uncrossed her legs and leaned forward to push my glass of water closer to me. "What? What do you mean they were there?"

"I know. I was as confused as you are. But we sat on the dock, danglin' our feet above the dark green water. Grandpa told me that true love doesn't have limits and that I need to tell

Wyatt how I feel about him." Goosebumps prickled my arms as I spoke about seeing them.

"Haven't we been tellin' you that for years?" Dad asked as he patted my leg.

I rolled my eyes and opened my mouth to respond, but a coughing fit came out instead. "Ouch." My throat felt as if it was being torn to shreds. I closed my eyes and lay my head against my pillow, my hands massaging my throat.

"You need to rest, Sis. It's not good to be talkin' so much," Dad told me.

I nodded, keeping my eyes closed.

There was a soft knock on the door. "Did she fall back into a coma?" Emelia whispered.

"No, she's just restin'," Mom said.

"I can hear you," I said, my voice sounding a little stronger. I opened my eyes and glanced over at Emelia. "Hi."

"Hey there. How are you feeling? You gave everyone quite the scare." Emelia rested her hand on top of mine.

"Better." I lifted myself to sit up straighter. "I have somethin' to tell ya."

"Dad and I are goin' to go grab some coffee. Give you two time to chat." Mom squeezed my ankle.

"What's up?" Emelia sat on a chair next to my bed, concern written all over her face.

"When I was in the coma . . . I know this is goin' to sound weird, but . . . I saw Quinn."

Emelia's eyebrows knitted together. "That's not funny, Caitlyn."

"I'm not tryin' to be. I'm bein' serious. She wanted me to tell you that she misses you and loves you. And Luke. And Tinkerbell. She said that God told her that He needed her up there, so that you could be up there, too. She said she likes it there, though. And then, she was gone." A tear dripped onto my hand. "But she could say her 'Ls.' She was really proud of that."

Emelia clutched her left hand over her heart as tears streamed down her face. "I don't know what to believe right now. But hearing that brings me so much peace and hope. Thank you."

I looked at her finger. *She's not wearin' the ring. What happened?* "Is Luke here?"

"Yes. He's right outside."

"I'd like to see him."

"Luke," Emelia called out.

He stood in the doorway with his hands in his pockets.

"I'll let you have some time with her." Emelia patted Luke's arm as he moved out of the way.

"Luke." I wanted to scream but knew it would tear my throat up. "You didn't ask her?"

"No. You were brought to the hospital on Valentine's Day, remember? I had my mind on you, not that."

"What are ya gonna do?"

"Her birthday is in June. I'm thinkin' I might ask her then." He scratched the back of his head.

"Promise me, Luke. Right now. That you will ask her. Soon."

"I will. I promise. I want nothin' more than to spend the rest of my life with her."

A knock sounded at the door. My eyes made their way across the room and landed on the most wonderful thing. Wyatt. My heart stopped in my chest. I had missed him more than he could possibly know. I had heard what he'd said in my ear. And I couldn't wait to tell him.

"What's with all the hushed voices in here?" Wyatt asked.

"Wyatt!" I grinned from ear to ear.

"I'll let you two have the room." Luke stood from the chair and started out of the room. "I'm so glad you're goin' to be okay."

"Me, too."

After Luke left the room, I motioned for Wyatt to sit. As he sat down, he started to speak, but I raised my index finger to his lips.

"Cowboy, I have so much I need to say. I'm sorry—"

"For what? You don't have anythin' to be sorry 'bout."

I thrust my hand toward him. "Yes. Yes, I do. I have somethin' I should have told you many years ago. First, though, I wanted to tell ya that I heard what ya said."

"What I said?"

"Yes. When ya whispered in my ear . . . that you love me and always have and always will."

His face turned as red as a beet. "Okay. Well, I meant every word."

"I know you did. I love you, too, Wyatt Grayson Glover. I have loved you since the first day I saw you. My grandpa told me that love has no limits, and I tried to put limits on my feelin's for you. I didn't want to burden you with all this." I motioned to the machines and the room.

"You do?" He bit his bottom lip. "But you could never be a burden to me, Chipmunk. Ever."

"I know. I learned a lot while I was in the coma. But the most important thing I learned is that I needed to tell ya that I love you, Cowboy. My heart about burst in my chest when I couldn't."

Wyatt stood and rested his hand along my jaw, his thumb skimming my cheek. His blue eyes bore into mine with an intensity I'd never seen before. "Let's do this the right way this time. I love you, Chipmunk."

He leaned in as I lifted my face to him. He lightly pressed his lips to mine. It was the best kiss I'd ever experienced. It was light. Gentle. Sweet. And held so much love and emotion.

When our lips parted, I said, "I love you, too, Cowboy."

Epilogue

Nine Months Later

Wyatt

I stood in front of the mirror, studying myself. It was an important night. I was taking Caitlyn to the Kickoff to Christmas Festival. But this time, as my date. My real one.

While Caitlyn had been in the hospital, my mother had relapsed and left again. I hoped I'd never see her again. She had taped another note to my cabin door. I didn't want to think about sad things on this night. It was too important.

Ever since Caitlyn was discharged from the hospital, we were inseparable. Just like old times. But this time, she was my girl, and I was her guy. She had a long road to a full recovery, but she had recovered completely within a few months. I was determined to make this night special for her. She needed it. She deserved it.

I slid my hand inside the pocket of my slacks. This was the first time I hadn't worn jeans in quite a while. I ran my fingers over the small box that was hidden there. My breath caught in my throat.

I wasn't sure if I'd chosen the right ring. A big stone for her would never do. She had never been into flashy things. But

I hoped the ring I picked was good enough for her. I hoped *I* was good enough for her.

I had asked Caitlyn's parents a few weeks ago for their blessing. What could I say? I wanted to do right by her in every way. Of course, they gave it wholeheartedly. Even Dyl offered his approval.

I sighed. "Here we go." I smiled at the man in the mirror, placed the hat Caitlyn had given me onto my head, and strode out the door.

* * *

Caitlyn

I smoothed the bottom of my knee-length, hot-pink dress. It had one shoulder strap with white stones going down and across the midsection and a sheer back with stones all over. Mom had taken me dress shopping when Wyatt asked me to be his date for the festival and told me to wear something nice. My blonde hair was wrapped into a bun.

After I stared at myself in the mirror, satisfied with the way I looked, I sat on my bed and slipped into my white, strappy heels. I hadn't worn heels since I'd been in a coma, so I was a little nervous about walking in them, but I was determined to do it.

Why does Cowboy want me to dress up? We go to this festival every year.

But this year was different. We weren't just friends anymore. The last nine months had been the hardest months of my life. But I had felt the most loved I had ever felt in my life, too. Wyatt was the one God had chosen for me. And I for him. I know because God and I had talked about it. A lot.

"Sis! Wyatt's here!" Mom yelled from downstairs.

"Comin'!"

I descended the stairs slowly, holding the railing. *Why didn't I pick more sensible shoes? Because this dress didn't call for sensible shoes, that's why.*

My eyes lifted to Wyatt standing at the bottom of the stairs with his hand held out to me. I placed my hand in his. "Wow," we both said at the same time as my feet hit the landing at the bottom of the staircase.

"That dress." He slowly twirled me around. "You look amazin'." He kissed my lips. I'd never tire of that. Never.

"Thank you." Heat scorched my cheeks. "You look very handsome."

He wore a blue plaid, long-sleeve shirt—plaid was his signature pattern. The blue in the shirt made his eyes brighter and brought out the flecks of gold that sometimes appeared in the center of them. He had on dark-brown pants and black cowboy boots. In his hand was the cowboy hat I'd gotten him for Christmas the year before. Not a single hair was out of place.

"Shall we go?" I suggested.

"Wait! Can I take a picture?" Mom asked with a giddy grin.

I rolled my eyes. "Mom, we aren't goin' to the prom."

Wyatt leaned in, kissed my cheek, and whispered, "Just let her take the picture."

"Fine."

Wyatt chuckled.

"Say cheese!"

* * *

Light turned to dusk, and the fireworks were getting ready to start. Everyone was there, including Uncle Colt and Aunt Callie along with Luke and Emelia. The twinkle lights sparkled against the heart-shaped ring on Emelia's left hand. I was so happy Luke finally asked her. And even more happy that she had said yes. Spencer and Jon were there, too, and Mom, Dad, and Dyl.

"The fireworks are one of my favorite parts," I said. I looked to my side where Wyatt had been standing, but he wasn't there. I twirled to see where he might have gone. He was beside me. On his knee. *What. Is. Happenin'?* My hands flew to my mouth. "Wyatt, what are you doin'?"

"Chipmunk, I fell in love with you the first time I laid eyes on you. The more I've gotten to know you over the years, the more my love has grown. We have wasted so much time livin' in fear and not spending our lives together. My love for you knows no limits. I want to spend the rest of my life lovin' you. So, Caitlyn LeeAnn Logan, will you make me the happiest man alive and marry me?"

My heart was pounding inside my chest. The fireworks had started, so I wasn't sure if it was my heart about to explode or the vibration of the fireworks. Wyatt opened the small, black velvet box in his hands and revealed a small pink and white diamond ring.

"YES! Of course, I'll marry you!" I squealed and threw myself into his arms with tears flowing down my cheeks.

We both stood as the crowd cheered loudly around us. Flashes of light went off. Wyatt, with shaking hands, removed the ring from the box and slid it onto my finger. I threw my arms around his neck and pressed my lips to his.

My fiancé. I could get used to that.

Available Soon . . .

JON AND LILI'S STORY
(*Edenton Bay Romance* Series, Book 4)

BY ELIZABETH WOODROW

Dear Reader:

Thank you for your interest in and purchase of Loving Without Limits (*Edenton Bay Romance* Series, Book 3). If you enjoyed this book, please be sure to obtain a copy of Jon and Lili's story in *Edenton Bay Romance* Series, Book 4, available soon at major book retailers.

Sincerely,

Elizabeth Woodrow

From the Author

Thank You from the Author

As this book's author, Elizabeth Woodrow, I sincerely thank you for your interest in and purchase of the book.

I hope you will please consider taking a moment to help other readers like you by leaving a rating or review of this book at your favorite online book retailer. You can do so by visiting the book's product page and locating the button for leaving a rating or review.

Thank you!

About the Author

Elizabeth Woodrow has loved writing since her first short story in first grade. In 2021, she made her dream come true with the publication of *Mending Broken Roads*, Book 1 in the *Edenton Bay Romance* Series. In 2022, her second novel, *Finding Redemption Ranch*, Book 2 in the *Edenton Bay Romance* Series, was brought into the world. Elizabeth crafts love stories with a faith-filled perspective, weaving heartfelt romance with the beauty of faith and starring plus-size characters. For updates about Elizabeth and her books, please be sure to follow her on Facebook (www.facebook.com/elizabeth.woodrow.author), Instagram (www.instagram.com/elizabeth.woodrow.author), or TikTok (www.tiktok.com/elizabeth.woodrow.author).